HyperLinkz

Hack Attack

BOOK 5 ROBERT ELMER

WATERBROOK
PRESS

HACK ATTACK
PUBLISHED BY WATERBROOK PRESS
2375 Telstar Drive, Suite 160
Colorado Springs, Colorado 80920
A division of Random House, Inc.

Unless noted in "The Hyperlinkz Guide to Safe Surfing," all Web-site names are fabrications of the author.

ISBN 1-57856-751-3

Published in association with the literary agency of Alive Communications, Inc., 7680 Goddard Street, Suite 200, Colorado Springs, CO 80920.

Library of Congress Cataloging-in-Publication Data
Elmer, Robert.
    Hack attack / Robert Elmer.—1st ed.
        p. cm.   (Hyperlinkz ; #5)
    Summary: Twelve-year-old Austin and Ashley Webster slip into the World Wide Web to research a school project and discover a frightening virus unleashed by a hacker.
    ISBN 1-57856-751-3
    1. Computer viruses—Fiction. 2. Internet—Fiction. 3. Christian life—Fiction. 4. Science fiction. I. Title.
PZ7.E4794Hac 2005
Fic—dc22   2004025728

Printed in the United States of America
2005—First Edition

10 9 8 7 6 5 4 3 2 1

Contents

Introducing...*Hack Attack* 1

1 Pompeii Problem 3

2 Ashley's Ashes 7

3 Busted 12

4 Grilled 17

5 The Plan 22

6 Clues in the Ashes 28

7 Danger at Spirit Lake 33

8 Jaunt to Jupiter 40

9 Virus 46

10 Art Class to the Rescue 51

11 Painting Pickle 59

12 Supposed to Be Mad 65

13 Webylonians 70

14 Oss-tin 76

15 Luther Link 82

16 Wormy Diet 87

17 Virus Patrol 92

18 Worm Gag 97

19 Who's the Rescuer? 102

20 Finding Graffiti Guy 106

21 Wrestling Match 110

22 Ashley's Plan 114

The Hyperlinkz Guide to Safe Surfing 118

Introducing... Hack Attack

Ashley Marie Webster here! Since my brother, Austin, has introduced the last two adventures, we agreed it would be my turn this time. Or we *will* agree as soon as he finds out. Meanwhile, I'll tell you what it's like to be sucked right into the Internet, just in case you've never been there.

I don't mean looking at a Web site from the Outside. And I don't mean clicking a mouse and watching everything on the screen from your chair. I'm talking about *really* being there.

I can't explain exactly how it works. Austin sure didn't mean for it to happen the first time he took my picture with a garage-sale digital camera plugged into his laptop computer. But there I went—the first of us to be sent online. And I have to say, that first time on the Web was pretty weird.

For starters I found out what it was like to be on the *Titanic* when it was sinking. (Hang on!) Austin visited the *Apollo 13* spacecraft on its way home from the moon. (Scary.) And we both got close to the action when the British navy was shooting cannonballs at Fort McHenry during the War of 1812. (Duck!)

I also found out that being on the Web is a lot like being here in the real world. When it's supposed to be cold, we're cold. We can feel the wind, smell the salt water—digital dust even makes me sneeze! While we are online, we seem just as digital as everything else.

So forget about being safe—not that I worry about that as much as my big brother. Fact is, I wasn't too nervous when we first met Ms. Mattie Blankenskrean on the Internet. She's actually from the same town as us—Normal, Illinois—though we didn't know it then.

Turns out she wasn't there to explore Web sites. She wanted to totally change them, at least when they didn't fit with her way of seeing things. A substitute teacher at my school, Chiddix Junior High, was up to the same thing—leave it to Austin to find that out. Mr. Z (really Raven Zawistokowski, but no one tries to say *that*) and Ms. B both work with a group called the Normal Council on Civil Correctness, or NCCC. It's their plan to take everything about Christian faith or Jesus off the Internet, making it seem as if the Bible is a big fairy tale you can skip reading if you want to. And when Austin and I got in their way...yikes! Things got nasty!

Not only did Mr. Z try to steal Austin's laptop and digital camera, which is rotten enough, but for the past few weeks, the guy has been following us in and out of the Web. Austin thinks that if he ever does catch up to us, he's going to make sure we don't get back to Normal again.

As for me, I'm hoping Mr. Z isn't that bad. But to tell you the truth, I'm not sure *what* he'll do.

CHAPTER 1

Pompeii Problem

Everybody knew how much Austin Webster liked to think things over before coming to a decision. He knew it. His sister, Ashley, knew it. Their Aunt Jessi knew it. Hey, no need to rush things, right? Except this time…

Ka-BOOM! As soon as Austin saw the digital cloud of steam and ash pop the top of Mount Vesuvius, he grabbed his sister and dove under a table inside the little sidewalk café. Maybe theirs wasn't the sturdiest building in the Roman city of Pompeii, but it would have to do.

"Everybody under the tables!" Austin yelled. A guy in a fancy knee-length robe looked down at him as if he were a rat collecting breadcrumbs.

No time to worry about that. Austin held his ears as the roar whooshed over the building and swept the street outside with a dragon's breath of fire and ash. Even the heavy tables inside the café were bowled away by the blast, like dice from the hand of a giant. Austin tried to hold Ashley's wrist as they tumbled into a wash of people, tables, chairs, and...

And a half-eaten onion the size of a baseball that came to rest on Austin's face.

"Anyone lose your lunch?" he asked. But this wasn't the time to joke. Everybody in the café had been thrown together into a pile, a groaning tangle of arms and legs and togas.

Togas, as in the Roman-style linen robes people wore.

"Ashley?" Austin called, and she pulled herself from the pileup at about the same time he did. He hoped he didn't look as dusty and dirty as she did.

His sister whispered to him what he already knew: "We need to get out of here now."

That would have been a fine idea. Only problem was somebody had suddenly turned out the lights. Outside the gaping hole of a window, a huge, inky shadow had turned day to night, just like that. Powdery gray ash rained down. When the floor shook once more, they both tumbled to their knees.

Austin grunted as he held up his camera. "Whoa, that one was really strong!" He tried to get to his feet, but the floor billowed and buckled below him like a wakeboard behind their grandpa's ski boat on Lake Winnebago.

"Hang on!" But to what? He tried to hold the wall next to him, which sorta kinda worked—until a big crack snaked down from the roofline, splitting the plaster.

"Yikes!" Austin stepped out into the street, but it was like stepping into a snowstorm. Except he could breathe in a snowstorm.

"Where's the"—*cough, cough*—"e-mail link?" Ashley asked from right behind him.

Pompeii's streets were set up in neat blocks, as if a Roman engineer with a straight ruler had designed the place. It shouldn't have been that hard to find the e-mail link, their escape route home.

But everything looked different now as closet-size shops stuffed full of sandals, embroidered Roman tunics, or spices leaned crazily over the narrow roads. To top it off, they had to wade through ankle-deep ash.

"This way." Austin covered his mouth and nose with the inside of his shirt, but it didn't help much. He fought for breath as Ashley stumbled along beside him. Good thing she held on to his arm; he could hardly see her in the ash blizzard.

"Where?" she gasped.

"The end of the block." Was that right? Well, he thought so. Nothing looked the same as it had even three minutes ago. They passed no one in the streets. Maybe everybody was hiding inside, and he didn't blame them. But if he and Ashley didn't find the link pretty soon...

Austin didn't want to think about it. He fell to his knees in the ash and dug like a dog for a bone. The link had to be here. Ashley tried to help, but she was coughing so hard he was afraid she was going to collapse.

Wait… No, his fingernails scraped against only cobblestones. Still, if this search worked, they would be able to feel what he'd hoped to see: the e-mail link that would send them back to the art-supply closet at Chiddix Junior High School in Normal, Illinois.

Ashley yelped before she disappeared, which was a very good thing.

"Thank you, God," Austin whispered before he crawled over to the spot where his sister had been digging. This had better work for him, too.

CHAPTER 2

AshLey's Ashes

"Hoo-doggy." Austin lay on his back, staring up at the ceiling, trying to catch his breath. "That was too close."

He shook his head and ash spilled out through the closet door into the classroom. Not that anybody would notice. The art room at Chiddix wasn't quite, well... The papier-mâché goop that had exploded last year from Melvin Overlake's piñata thing was still there, dried on the ceiling. And the floor around the pottery wheel wasn't exactly spotless either.

Ashley was staring at herself in the small mirror on the inside of the room's closet door.

"You look like..."—he stood up behind her to take a look—"like one of those mummies in the monster movies."

"Thanks." She tried to wipe the ash from her eyes. "You, too."

"So did you get the pictures you needed?"

She pulled out her "Shots to Get" checklist from a jeans pocket—Roman mosaic, sculpture, graffiti (but not the rude kind). All were pictures she needed for her advanced art-class project.

"Got 'em. But how did that happen? Didn't you tell me we had twenty minutes before the volcano was supposed to blow?"

Austin shook his head. "Guess the programming was unstable."

"Unstable? What's that supposed to mean?"

"It speeds up; it slows down. The colors change, or the site freezes up. All kinds of funky stuff. Makes it hard to know exactly what's going on."

But then it hit him. He stared at his sister.

"Whoa. Wait a minute." He wasn't sure she would care, but this was weird. "It's never happened like this before."

"What, that we almost got killed? I thought you and Drew came pretty close when you went to *www-dot-tornadochaser-dot-com.*"

Okay, so his friend wasn't much of a driver. "That's not what I'm talking about. We've never been able to bring anything back with us from the Web. Always before we've left it all behind, back on the Internet."

"Wish we had this time, too." Ashley combed her hair

with her fingers and glanced down at her watch. "I could do without souvenir volcanic ash."

"Yeah, but don't you see?" This meant something, Austin was sure. "The programming is changing. Somebody must be messing with it."

"Is that why you were running all over the place before the volcano blew?"

Austin had no idea what she was talking about.

"Running all over? No. I went right to the link, made sure it was working, and came straight back to meet you. What do you mean?"

"Oh, come on. First you were ahead of me—even looked right at me—and then you hid behind a vegetable cart. You kept playing peekaboo like that for a few minutes, till suddenly you stopped and jogged up behind me. Then the volcano let loose."

Austin scratched his head. "That's wacko. You sure it was me?"

"Are you saying it wasn't? Who else at *www-dot-PompeiiExplodes-dot-com* was wearing blue jeans and an Einstein T-shirt? Your clone?"

Austin took a deep breath and coughed. "That's just the kind of thing I mean. I think something weird's happening online. And I'm *sure* we had twenty minutes before the thing was supposed to blow."

"Maybe you figured wrong."

"No way. I did the math twice. I'm positive I was right."

"Well, let me know when you find what went wrong. Meantime, I'm going to stop by Jessi's house on the way home and clean up. You'd better too, or Mom's going to wonder what happened to us."

"Why not tell Mom we were playing in a volcano?"

Ashley didn't laugh. "And dinner's in an hour, unless your watch is still slow."

But Austin's watch wasn't slow, not since he'd set it yesterday to the U.S. Naval Observatory clock at *www.time.gov.*

As they left the art room, he tried not to get volcanic dust on his laptop. The camera could use a good cleaning, though.

Needing to get a couple homework papers out of his locker, Austin took the long way around, through the school's deserted halls, hoping he wouldn't run into anybody. Of course, by five in the afternoon everyone should have gone home, except maybe Mr. Witherwax, the janitor. So that was probably him making a strange noise just around the corner, sounding very much like someone shaking a spray can.

Ka-chicka-chicka-chicka… Pffffffft!

Austin slowed at the end of the dark hall. Maybe somebody was touching up the new mural Ashley and her art class had painted on the wall at the end of the hallway. The "I Have a Dream" mural had the Wright brothers flying in from the left, a space shuttle taking off on the right, and a big picture of Martin Luther King Jr. in the middle, preaching up a storm.

Yeah, that's gotta be it, Austin thought. Only wasn't the mural done already? And who would be working on it there in the shadows, anyway?

CHAPTER 3

Busted

Austin hugged the wall, slipping up to the corner without a sound. From what he could hear, he was pretty sure somebody was messing with the new mural. What kind of turkey would want to do that?

A not-very-tall turkey. Leaning around the corner, Austin noticed the vandal was wearing the same jeans and Einstein T-shirt he was. Weird…he'd never seen anybody else wearing this shirt. The guy even had the same haircut. And whoever he was, he was working on a dark mustache for Martin Luther King Jr. He'd already scribbled the word *Austin* across the space shuttle.

He can't do that! Austin felt his face heating up, but he pulled back to think for a moment. Now what? Go for help? No, the vandal would be gone by the time they got back. Plus, then he'd have to explain what he himself was doing in the school building this late.

Get Ashley? That would take too long too. And what could she do that he couldn't? He looked down at his digital camera and had an idea. Quickly he blew off much of the volcanic dust and stepped out from his hiding place.

"Hey, you!" He made his voice as deep as he could. "Knock it off!"

Austin figured it should have gone like this: Step one—surprise the bad guy so he turns around. Step two—snap his picture for the police. Step three—run like crazy.

Instead, it went like this: Step one—surprise the bad guy. Step two—try to look through the viewfinder, which was all clouded up with volcanic dust. Step three—wonder what happened.

Actually, Austin did manage to snap a couple blind shots, but he had no idea if he was pointed at the right thing. They could have been closeups of the guy's shoes, for all he knew. But that hardly mattered when he lowered the camera.

For a second he thought he was looking in a mirror—same face, same clothes, same everything. And that couldn't have been right. He blinked to be sure, but things were happening too fast to understand.

"Give me that camera!" The other boy didn't wait, just grabbed—and missed. He used his can of black spray paint like a weapon, missing Austin's face only by a few inches.

Pffft!

Austin ducked and hollered and managed to grab the paint can to keep it from spraying him, which almost worked. He caught some black spray in the right eye, and it burned like fire. After a short tug of war, he managed to pry the can out of the kid's hand.

Take that! That'll teach you to paint mustaches on Dr. King. That'll teach you to mess with Austin T. Webster!

Funny thing was, the fight was over almost before it began, and the vandal slipped away and out the door, leaving Austin slumped against the ruined mural, just as footsteps pounded down the hallway. Perfect timing, right?

When Mr. Witherwax saw Austin, his eyes nearly popped out of his bald head.

"Drop the paint where you are, boy." He tucked a rag into his back pocket and pulled out a cell phone.

Austin couldn't make his legs move as he stared down at the can of glossy black spray paint in his hand. He did as he was told. But...

"He's getting away!" Austin pointed at the double doors as he rose to his feet, still wobbly kneed. "The guy who did it... I saw him. I stopped him."

"No, you don't." Mr. Witherwax moved quickly to block the exit. Most people wouldn't guess he'd be able to move that fast. He stood there in front of the doorway, arms crossed over his barrel of a chest, staring down at Austin with his eyebrows pointed into sharp triangles. Anybody could see he wasn't buying it.

"Wouldn't have thought it of you." He looked more sad than anything else.

"But…" Austin couldn't believe what was happening. The other guy had to be hustling off across the track oval just outside the double doors, leaving the mural and Austin's face and hands splattered with black paint. The mural was ruined, and somebody was going to be in big trouble for it. It all looked very, very bad.

What was he going to say? *Go after somebody wearing, uh, jeans like mine and a T-shirt with a picture of Albert Einstein on the front, just like, uh, this one. Oh yeah. And the guy's about my height and weight, with the same color hair too.*

He couldn't say that.

"Wait, I can prove it wasn't me." Austin had reached full-stage panic. "I took a picture of him, just so I could…"

No, wait. Suddenly it didn't seem like such a good idea to show anyone the photo. But when he looked down at the camera, he realized he had already squeezed the View button, so he hit Cancel a bunch of times.

"Show it to Mr. Hayward when he gets here." That would be Mr. Hayward, the principal. Mr. Witherwax looked out over his shoulder through the glass of the door before he pointed at the floor. "Meanwhile, you sit down right there and wait."

He keyed in a number on his cell phone and waited for an answer.

Who was the janitor calling? The police?

Austin punched a couple more buttons on his camera, just to check. The green light on the side of the camera started blinking, as if it was downloading an image to the Internet. He'd seen that before.

Uh-oh. Can anything else go wrong?

"You've gotta believe me." Austin gave up trying to stop the download and sat down. "I know it looks bad, but I really didn't do anything."

"You're right about it looking bad." The janitor held up a finger as someone finally came on the line for him.

"Yeah, Mr. Hayward? Lonnie Witherwax down here at the school. Uh, mostly fine, sir. But we do have a problem, and I think you're going to want to come down here right away. No, nothing like that. But I've caught a vandal who spray-painted graffiti all over the new mural…. No, I'm not kidding. And I think you're going to have a hard time believing who did it too. Uh…maybe you'd better come down and see for yourself, sir."

Austin closed his eyes and tried to pretend this wasn't for real. First a volcano erupts early and nearly kills him and his sister. Then he runs into a crazy look-alike vandal and gets blamed for something terrible he didn't even do.

Could it get any worse?

CHAPTER 4

Grilled

"I'd like to believe you, Austin, but…"

The Chiddix Junior High principal paced behind his desk, holding his two chins with one hand while Austin squirmed in a rock-hard wooden chair.

But what?

Well…

One: Austin was covered in spray paint.

Two: The janitor had caught him holding a half-empty can of paint, with nobody else in sight.

Three: The vandal had written *Austin* across the mural.

Four: Austin couldn't describe the person who had really done it, which made his explanation sound like a lame, made-up excuse.

Five: He wasn't supposed to be in the school building that late, anyway, though kids in sports did it all the time, no big deal. Teachers didn't worry about it too much, as long as you had a good reason. But today…

Wasn't that already enough to bury him?

His eye was still stinging from the spray paint, and he was still dusted in ash, though he'd tried to brush most of it off. But those were the least of his worries. His mind spun as he tried to figure out what to say, how to step out of the path of this train wreck.

"You say you were getting some homework out of your locker, and you heard the sound of someone spraying."

"Yes sir." Austin knew his story wasn't holding up very well, if at all. No matter that it was true. "You know how a can of paint sounds when someone's shaking it…that—"

"You don't have to demonstrate." Mr. Hayward held up his hand. "I know what you're talking about. But you said that when you saw what was happening with the mural, you tried to take a picture of the vandal."

"That's right."

Austin wasn't sure why he was telling that part of the story, true as it was. He knew where it would take them—and that it would be no help.

"But now the photo is gone."

Austin sighed. "Right. I pressed the wrong button, and it started to download—well, it's gone now."

"How convenient."

"It's not like it sounds."

How *did* it sound? And where had he sent the person he'd downloaded over the school wireless network? To a Web site? Maybe that's why Mr. Witherwax hadn't seen anyone outside, running away. Because by that time the vandal really *hadn't* been outside anymore.

But Austin would have to worry about that later. Mr. Hayward had questions of his own.

"And can you tell me where you were before this... incident?"

"Um...I was with my sister, Ashley. She left for home right before I was going to. We were doing some research for her art project."

"Here in the school? Even when you know it's locked and off limits after four o'clock?"

"We were sort of...I mean, not exactly."

"Not exactly?" Mr. Hayward parked his hands on his hips, and his face started turning colors, kind of like the bad programming back at *www.PompeiiExplodes.com*. Orange to red to purple. "Austin, don't you understand how serious this is? I should be calling the police. We're talking about malicious mischief. Vandalism. People get arrested for this kind of thing. You need to come clean with me."

"Yes sir. I know, sir." Austin's head was still spinning, and he couldn't stop it even by holding it. "I'm really sorry about being in the building when I wasn't supposed to be. I won't do it again. But I didn't ruin the mural. Honest, I didn't."

That's when Austin's mom arrived at the office, and the shocked look on her face reminded Austin of how he himself must have looked when he saw the vandal. This was all too bizarre.

"I'm sure there's a good explanation for this." Mrs. Webster's voice was soft, as tears floated in her clear, blue eyes. She dabbed at them with a tissue from her purse. Of course, she had to hear everything, which meant Mr. Witherwax had to give his side of the story again. Though mostly quiet, the janitor had stayed in the office too.

"I seen nobody else, ma'am. I even looked out through the door and out at the field, just to give your boy the benefit of the doubt, right? If there was anybody running away, the way he said there was, I would've seen him. But I didn't. Your son was the only person in the building when I came on him."

Mrs. Webster looked over at Austin as if waiting for his side of the story, but all he could do was open and close his mouth. This ship was sinking fast.

"Austin, you've never done anything like this before." By this time the color in Mr. Hayward's cheeks had returned to near normal, and he sounded as if he was trying to wrap things up. "Even so, we're going to be taking this offense very seriously. For now I'm suspending you from school for the rest of the week—Wednesday, Thursday, and Friday—but I want you and both your parents to meet me back here in my office at 3:00 tomorrow afternoon."

Suspended. Oh wow. Austin's mouth went dry and his stomach went woozy as the principal went on.

"If you're not prepared to bring me an apology and a plan to make things right, we'll have to discuss a harsher consequence. Do you understand?"

"Yes sir." Austin understood. The hammer was coming down, and he knew only one way out of this horrible mess.

Find the real vandal.

And fast.

CHAPTER 5

The Plan

Ashley shivered as she helped her mom clear the supper dishes that night, but not because it was cold. When Dad crossed his arms and stared down at the tablecloth that way, she had a pretty good idea what was coming. Sort of like the steam around Vesuvius before it let loose.

Not that her dad had a hot temper. Just the opposite, really. And most of the time Ashley really liked her family's dessert discussions around the dinner table. When Dad didn't have to work a late shift at the Normal Medical Center, they could sit here for hours, talking about what was happening at school or at youth group or discussing a good book, or even a verse from the Bible.

But not tonight. Tonight Ashley held her breath as she slid back into her seat.

Her dad combed his fingers through what was left of his

hair. "All right, Austin. I talked to Mr. Hayward on the phone. Now you tell me your side of the story."

So Austin told how they'd been working on Ashley's project, how he'd heard the spray painter when he'd returned to his locker before leaving—all that. And the whole time Dad sat there with his arms crossed, tapping his foot and frowning.

"That still doesn't explain what you were doing in the building so late."

"Mr. Freedlander sometimes gives us permission."

"Including today?"

Austin squinted as if he was definitely feeling the heat. In a way, Ashley wished he would just tell their parents everything—how they'd somehow gotten into the Internet and could visit Web sites. Maybe they should at least *try* to explain, the way they had tried once before.

But it hadn't worked then. The truth was just too weird. And she guessed Austin wouldn't spill the beans tonight either, not when it would make his story sound even stranger than it already did.

"I'm not lying, Dad," Austin pleaded. At least he could say that. "I really didn't do anything to the mural. How could I? Ashley and everybody put all that work into it."

Their dad nodded and closed his eyes. "I know. You have to admit, though, your story sounds pretty…far out."

If he only knew.

"But you believe me, don't you?" Austin looked from his dad to his mom. "Both of you believe me, right?"

"We believe you," answered his mom. "But can't you explain what happened a little better to your principal? Your story just sounds so…odd."

By this time Ashley was dying. She had to say something.

"I feel like this is all my fault. Austin was helping *me* with an art assignment when he didn't want to. I talked him into it."

Her brother turned to her with a surprised look on his face.

"Why didn't you wait for him, then, Ashley?"

She gulped.

"I had to stop by Jessi's on the way home. Austin said for me to go ahead. We had no idea this would happen."

"Obviously not."

"All we can do now is tell Mr. Hayward what really happened, right, Dad?"

Their father held up his hands and sighed. "You've certainly gotten yourselves into some trouble, kids, by being in the wrong place at the wrong time. But tomorrow we'll all go in to see Mr. Hayward together."

"Meanwhile, there's somebody out there with black paint on his hands." Ashley marched around her room that night after dinner. "And we're going to find out who it is!"

Her Aunt Jessi sat on the bed while Austin stared out the window at the streetlight. He got like that sometimes when he was thinking.

And, yes, Jessi was *Aunt* Jessi, as in their mother's baby sister. Though it didn't happen that way very often, their aunt was their age, and she went to Chiddix Junior High too. Applet, her beagle, had plunked down on the throw rug next to the bed, her ears flopped out to the sides.

"We're going to find him," added Ashley, her voice louder than it probably should have been. But right now she figured a little extra volume might make up for the fact that she didn't really know what she was talking about. "And we're going to prove Austin didn't do it."

She jabbed her finger in the air to make her point.

"Preach it, sister!" Jessi's blond hair flew around her head as she jumped to her feet and cheered. Applet woke up from her doggy dream to look at them and wag her tail. "But how are we going to do that?"

"Give me a minute to think."

So while Ashley thought, Austin stared.

"I know!" Jessi smiled. "We could check everybody's hands tomorrow at school."

Austin shook his head without looking at them.

"Why not?" Jessi asked.

"For one thing, I don't know for sure if he got black paint on his hands. I think so, but I'm not one hundred percent."

"Well…" Jessi clearly wasn't going to let picky details stop her.

"For another thing, this guy probably isn't going to be at school tomorrow, especially if he's still on the Web, where I sent him."

Both Ashley and Jessi were quiet for a minute or two.

"You sent him onto the Internet?" Jessi whispered.

"Pretty sure," he told the window.

"Whoa." Jessi stared at her nephew. "That's extreme. He's probably freaked out."

"He probably is." Austin leaned his head against the window frame, sounding tired and bummed.

"Okay, so are you thinking we have to rescue this guy?" Ashley wanted to know. "How come?"

"What do you mean, 'how come?'" Austin whirled around. "So maybe he's a juvenile delinquent or a weirdo or whatever. But I still can't zap him to who-knows-where and then forget about it."

"I didn't say to do that." Ashley held up her hands.

"Hey, don't worry." Jessi bounced back onto the bed. "If you're really that worried, all we have to do is jump back into the Net and grab anyone with black paint on his hands who's not supposed to be there."

This time Austin and Ashley looked at each other, and Ashley guessed they were both thinking the same thing. Austin was the first to say something, though.

"Not a bad idea, Jess."

"Really?" She flinched as if he had splashed ice water in her face. "You think so?"

"Sure, I think so. But…we need somebody out here, watching the monitor. Watching for the guy."

She brightened at that. "Like directing traffic? Saying where to go?"

"Sort of. Here, let me show you what you have to do."

CHAPTER 6

CLues iN the Ashes

"This is creepy." Ashley looked around while her brother bent down to check out the set of footprints leading away from where they stood. "Almost as if we're on the moon."

"This is the same place we were before." Austin's voice sounded pretty shaky.

"You're sure?" This time Ashley knew he couldn't be right. "Everything's different. No city. No people. No nothing. Only miles and miles of dusty ash, though I guess there's still a mountain."

"No, it's the same place. We're standing on top of the city, is all. I think this part of the Web site shows things a few years after the eruption."

"Oh." Ashley got it now, but that only creeped her out even more. "So that means everybody is…"

"Yeah." Austin straightened up and dusted off his knees. "I just wonder what happened to the vandal."

"Well, don't we just follow the footprints? Shouldn't they belong to him?"

"I think so. But what I don't understand is why they bee-line off to…"—he shaded his forehead with a hand and squinted toward the east—"to wherever he went."

Wherever he had gone, Austin and Ashley now followed, trying not to kick up too much volcanic dust. Even if it was just a Web site, Ashley felt weird about walking on top of a lost city buried by a volcano.

"So here's the thing," her brother told her. "Let's pretend you've never been on the Internet before, and now all of a sudden you're here. What do you do? Where do you go?"

Ashley thought about it for a second before shrugging. "I don't know. It's pretty confusing."

"Exactly!" He pointed down at the footprints in the dust. "So now look at these tracks. Do they look like they were made by someone who's lost and doesn't know where he's going?"

"Not exactly. So—"

"So I'm guessing this guy has been here before. The question is, how?"

They kept following the tracks across the gray desert, toward the mountain and up a slow rise. Ashley thought she could see a few links up ahead, which would give them—or the guy they were following—a way out of this dead world. Austin must have spotted the flashing, bright red writing too, though it was too far away to read. Suddenly something soft brushed up against Ashley's leg, like a little lost lamb, and she giggled.

"What's funny?" Austin glanced around for the joke.

A chime went off somewhere above their heads. *Brrriiing!* Ashley looked straight down at a batch of bright purple words floating and bobbing around her knee like puppy dogs begging for someone to chase them.

jessi465: u there, guys?

"Oh, *there* she is." Austin bent down and squinted at the words. "I was wondering when we'd hear from her."

"That's Jessi?" The words tickled Ashley's ankles before they faded and disappeared.

"Yeah." He patted one of the words the way he would pat Applet. "I set her up with instant messaging so she can tell us what's going on out there, or what she sees. She types in IM, but we talk back. Voice recognition. The cool thing is that the computer translates what we say into IM language that appears on the computer screen."

jessi465: u ok? all I see r u + footprints.

"We're fine." Austin hollered at the purple words. "Tell…us…where…the…footprints…go."

jessi465: U DONT HAV 2 YELL. I HEAR U FINE.

"Oh. Okay." Austin lowered his voice but still talked directly at the words. "I wasn't sure how well it was going to work from our end, or if anybody else was going to be able to hear us too. So tell us which way—"

jessi465: this is 2 cool! u r in there and im out here, but now we can IM. hi ashley whats up?

"Yeah, Jess." Austin frowned. "But can you tell us which—"

jessi465: can we get all our friends online, 2? do u think we can all talk at the same time?

"JESSI!"

They waited a minute for Jessi to get over it.

jessi465: sorry...keep going to top of hill, then turn left.

Ashley looked up as the chimes sounded again. This time red-and-white-striped letters bounced into the mix.

hammerjeff3: hey whats up? is austin online?

Brrriiing!

Still more letters appeared, pink and polka-dotted with tiny blue smiley faces.

superfreckles: duz nybody no where ashleys hiding? i thot we could study 4 the math quiz 2nite.

Ashley looked at her brother and laughed.

"Cool idea, Austin. Looks like Jeff and Amie know where to find us now. Probably half the rest of the school too." Or at least everybody who was on IM.

hammerjeff3: nybody hear wht happend @ school 2nite?? I herd mr hayward was running from his car.

Austin groaned and held his forehead. Ashley sighed. Already the rumor machine was in high gear. No telling where it would stop.

"Let's go, Austin." Ashley whispered as she tugged his sleeve. "We can talk to everybody later. We have to find that guy."

So they took off at a run across the ash heap that had been Pompeii, trying not to kick up too much dust as they followed the trail of footprints. A purple instant message bounced in front of their feet, and Ashley almost fell on her face.

Actually, she looked down just in time to read it—but not in time to do anything about it.

jessi465: hey! go around...looks like u r just about 2 step on a link!

CHAPTER 7

Danger at Spirit Lake

⌖

"Wow." Austin caught his breath at the other end of the link. No more volcanic dust here. And except for losing the trail, he couldn't complain about the change of scenery. Instead, he filled his lungs with the misty lake breeze, looked down at the canoe paddle in his hands, and smiled.

"Yeah, this is more like it." Ashley returned his smile from her seat at the back of the canoe and dipped her hand in the clear blue water. "But I don't know what this has to do with Pompeii and Vesuvius."

"I have no idea either." Austin leaned over the side of the canoe to read the stenciled lettering: Spirit Lake Resort.

Cool. This lake and these woods were a little like parts of Wisconsin, with tall green fir trees all around, carpeting the hills like green was one of God's favorite colors. Unlike Wisconsin, though, a snowcapped mountain sparkled in the early morning sunlight as it towered over the far end of the lake. A rustic log lodge nestled against the eastern shore. *Perfect.*

"Maybe the link is the mountain," Ashley wondered aloud. "Like Vesuvius was on that site, and here there's a mountain too—whatever it's called. Do you think?"

"The mountain..." Something stirred at the back of Austin's mind, like half of an answer to a trivia question during a Chiddix Knowledge Bowl competition. He looked down at the side of the canoe once more. *Spirit Lake Resort.* The name reminded him of something; he just wasn't quite sure what.

"One thing's for sure." Ashley leaned back and sighed. "I don't think we've ever been to a prettier Web site. This lake is great."

"Yeah, this lake." By this time Austin was seriously working the back alleys of his brain, poking through his memories, and the feeling he should know this place was getting stronger with every stroke of his paddle. "We should get back to the resort over there."

"Relax, Austin." Ashley didn't seem to share his concern. "Have you ever been anywhere this gorgeous?"

He hadn't, but something was not right here in paradise. And Austin was pretty sure it didn't have anything to do with catching up to his spray-painting look-alike. Or did it? Worried, he checked the other side of the canoe.

"You're going to tip us over!" Ashley waved at him. "Sit down!"

"Look." Austin pointed at the right outer side of the canoe as if he had just seen a ghost. And maybe he had, in a way.

"Oh my." Ashley's jaw dropped when she leaned out far enough to see *Austin was here* sprayed down the side of the aluminum canoe, from the bow to the stern, and upside-down as if the person had painted it while sitting inside the boat.

"He was here." Austin wondered now what had happened to the kid they'd been chasing and how close they'd come to landing right on top of him. How had he linked out of there before they arrived?

"And he could have gone anywhere." Ashley pointed to the links that had just now appeared all around them—some in the water, some right out in the air.

Top Ten Most Powerful Volcanoes.

Volcano Trivia Contest.

Exploding Hawaiian Volcanoes!

Volcanoes in the Solar System.

These links didn't sound very promising. Austin looked around him one more time, trying to jog the memory loose. *Spirit Lake, Spirit Lake.* He knew this one. He nearly bit his tongue when he finally remembered.

"I think I know where we are, Ashley."

"Where?" She looked as clueless as before.

"This is Washington State, and that"—he pointed up at the pretty mountain with the blade of his paddle—"is Mount St. Helens."

Bing-bing-bing! A bell rang somewhere, and a digitized voice said, "Correct!"

"Who said that?" Austin asked, but nobody answered. As they drifted closer to the lodge, even more links popped into view.

Mount St. Helens Xtreme Tours.

Mount St. Helens Visitors Center.

And a dozen other touristy kinds of things.

Ashley scrunched her nose the way their dad did when they tried to explain to him the differences between the bands they listened to.

"Okay, so…"

"So if that's Mount St. Helens and this is Spirit Lake… Ashley, Mount St. Helens had one of the hugest volcanic eruptions ever, back in May of 1980."

Bing-bing-bing! The bell again. "Correct!" said the Web voice. This was getting annoying.

But now they faced at least one more big question, and Austin knew it was on his sister's mind, too.

"The only question is," he told her, "how much time is this site going to give us before the mountain explodes?"

He followed Ashley's gaze to a bright pull-down banner with a sideways thermometer and a counter.

" 'Seconds to the next eruption,' " he read aloud. " 'Reloading graphics. One hundred seconds. Ninety-nine. Ninety-eight…' "

Yikes.

"Oh man." Ashley rubbed her forehead. "Haven't we already done this once today?"

Austin glanced at the links again, wondering which was the quickest way to get out of there. Because he now remembered seeing pictures of Spirit Lake choked with blown-down trees, as dead and gray after the eruption as it was at this second alive and blue. He slapped at a tickle on the back of his neck, expecting a mosquito but feeling instead a squishy mess of…what, exactly?

"Ooh, gross, Austin." Ashley must have seen what attacked him. "Looks like somebody dumped a bowl of purple alphabet soup all over the back of your neck."

Austin looked at his hand, now covered with purple letters. Bits and pieces of IM-spelled things like *jessi465:* and *www.st-helens-blast.com* and *blow up.*

"Say that again?" Austin yelled and looked over his shoulder at the pretty mountain that wasn't going to be pretty for much longer. Maybe they should have tried to link somewhere else…maybe someplace that wasn't going to explode in a minute and a half.

"I'd be glad to." A guy in a green windbreaker dropped down from somewhere above their heads, riding a bright yellow banner ad. "These high-quality ceramics are made of genuine Mount St. Helens' ash, handcrafted here in Washington State and available for the Internet-only special price of just—"

"Bad timing." Austin tried to ignore the Web ad for tacky souvenirs and paddled hard for shore—or a link. Most of the links seemed to stay just out of reach.

Jessi finally bounced back with an IM.

jessi465: i just checkd out ur site u guys. if i were u id get out of there asap. oh but if u have time could u bring me back a flower vase made of ash?

"Forget the souvenir, Jessi!" Ashley dug her paddle into the water so hard it nearly bent. "Just get us out of here! Push the button!"

Isn't that why they had left her behind?

"I don't know what she's doing." Austin shook his head and raised his voice. "Jessi, you've got to start the Mail Retrieve program, the way we set it up. Now would be good."

They paddled for shore as a few more seconds passed. Twenty-nine, twenty-eight…

"Jessi!" Ashley yelled.

jessi465: im trying im trying…which program did u say?

"Oh brother." Austin looked around again. Maybe they should paddle right through one of the links they'd seen before. *If we can reach one.*

"This way!" Ashley must have had the same idea, and they both headed straight for a glowing yellow headline floating a few inches above the water's surface. Never mind what it said. Anywhere else would be fine.

Anywhere.

CHAPTER 8

Jaunt to Jupiter

Well, *almost* anywhere else would have been fine. But a moment later Ashley almost wished she was back in the comfy canoe on the lake that was about to be blasted by Mount St. Helens.

"What are we doing now?" Like a dog dangling at the end of a leash, she held on to the end of a twenty-foot-long antenna-like pole as it swung her slowly around in circles. The other end of the antenna plugged into a space probe about the size of a small sports car. Two large satellite dishes sprouted from the sides of the satellite. Austin held on to the antenna too, and he seemed to be staring at something.

"Somebody's been here before us, Ashley." He jerked his head toward the side of the probe, where someone had spray-painted a big smiley face.

"Who would do that?" she asked.

Austin shook his head. "Take a guess," he told her. "But

whoever it was is nowhere in sight now." He eyed the space probe again and whistled. "Man, I never thought I'd see a space probe up close like this. This is so cool."

"This is so *not* cool." Ashley's stomach was starting to feel the spin of *www-dot-lets-spin-around-in-outer-space-and-get-sick-to-our-stomachs-dot-com*. Well, that's what she would have named the site.

"Are you kidding?" Austin was still sounding pretty excited. "We're hanging on to the *Galileo* space probe that went to Jupiter and took all kinds of pictures of its moons. Check it out."

He pointed at the main body of the space probe, the part with all the gizmos and the weird spray-paint job. When he did, a balloon popped up with a *swoosh*, reminding Ashley of the word balloons in comic strips.

This is the ultraviolet spectrometer, read the first balloon. Austin pointed at the end of another smaller antenna.

These are the radioisotope thermoelectric generators, the next balloon told them.

Whatever.

Austin would have kept going all day if Ashley hadn't stopped him. "And we got here from that pretty lake because?"

"Because look down there."

He pointed past his feet toward the surface of a golden, cratered planet. Beyond lay another huge planet, this one striped, but it looked as if there was enough to watch on the smaller globe. Below their feet, dozens—no, hundreds—of geysers spewed yellow clouds, bright orange fountains of lava, and steam that drifted slowly and left a thick haze on the surface. And though Ashley still held on for dear life to the spinning antenna, she couldn't help staring at the incredible fireworks show.

"Io." Austin announced the word as if Ashley should have known what it meant. As in, *I owe* my sister a huge apology when we get home, if we ever get home. But that wasn't what he meant.

Ashley just stared as he explained.

"Io is one of Jupiter's moons and the most volcanic place in the whole solar system. Tons and tons of volcanoes—scientists think it's because Jupiter's gravity jerks it around so much. The moon's insides get smashed around and heated up, and—"

Boooom! An extralarge volcano down on the surface let loose at that exact moment. Ashley could feel the explosion rumbling in her chest. But then she realized something stranger still.

"How come we don't need spacesuits to be out here?" she asked. "Usually on other sites we've felt cold or hot or wet or whatever, like we would if we went to that place in real life. But this is different."

"I don't know." Austin frowned as he thought. "We must have linked to a NASA Web site, or something like it. But we're breathing and talking like normal out here."

Ashley didn't much care what the explanation was. In fact, except for getting dizzy from the constant spinning, she couldn't complain too much, after all. The view was pretty amazing, and as long as they got home okay and this *Galileo* thing didn't—

"Do you feel that?" Austin studied the main body of the probe, with all of its scanners and spectrometers and modules and detectors and whatnots. Everything looked okay to Ashley, but she'd felt it too—a jerking stop and start.

"Maybe the ride's over," Ashley guessed. "Do we have to put in another fifty cents? And don't you think Jessi should have caught up to us by now?"

"Yeah, but who knows? Maybe she got sidetracked on a home-shopping site."

"She did not." Ashley had to defend their aunt, even if Austin was right. "I'm sure she's going to show up any second."

And that would be good. They hung on as the antenna kept spinning, but now instead of simply giving a little jerk once in a while, it creaked and groaned as it made its way around.

"It's spinning faster," announced Austin matter-of-factly. He was right. In almost no time, the antenna had sped up, and

Ashley was glad she had pulled herself up on it. Now she was riding the antenna as if it were a bull at a rodeo.

"It's getting worse!" she called over to Austin.

"Maybe we're dragging down its orbit, messing with its path or something—"

"What does that mean?" she wanted to know.

"We're getting closer to Io."

Which, of course, meant closer to the volcanoes. *Terrific.* Ashley couldn't guess what that might mean here or how close they would actually have to get before they were barbecued. Because however easy it was to breathe on this site, the volcanic action looked pretty real to life. By this time sweat was trickling down her forehead, and her tennis shoes were feeling plenty toasty. The heat was on.

Ashley closed her eyes and hoped not to see another volcano for a very long time.

"I should have stayed behind." Austin was getting flushed in the face—or maybe it was just the glow from the volcanoes below. "I could have worked the computer for us."

"And sent me here alone, or with Jessi?" Ashley shook her head. "I don't think so."

jessi465: hey what wud have been wrong w/that? i travel fine.

Ashley had never been so glad to see purple IM letters, or to hear the chime that announced them. But that didn't mean the cavalry had come to the rescue.

"Okay, Jessi." Austin jumped into action as the letters bumped into *Galileo* and floated away. "Let's go through those steps I wrote down for you."

jessi465: i did all ur steps 3 times and still nothing. not my fault.

"Nobody says it's your fault, Jess," Ashley spoke up. "Can't you try again, please?"

jessi465: u guys look like a circus act. ROFL.

Well, Ashley sure wasn't Rolling On the Floor Laughing. Why did it always come down to the last seconds like this?

jessi465: sorry. its just lately u get 2 go 2 all the cool places.

"Trade you next time."

jessi465: no kidding?

"No kidding. Now, would you please try Austin's program again? 'Cause believe me, this place is getting less and less cool all the time."

CHAPTER 9

Virus

"Are you kids still doing homework in there?" Austin's mom's voice drifted up the stairway. Austin's hands felt as if they'd melted into permanent claws after hanging on to the *Galileo* antenna for so long. At least Jessi had come through this time.

She gave Ashley a high-five, and Austin checked his watch. Five to nine.

"I'm just leaving." Jessi started for the door.

"Oh, I didn't mean it that way, little sis." Mrs. Webster came up the stairs as she spoke. "You guys have been so quiet, I was starting to wonder."

She appeared in the doorway, and Jessi gave her a hug as she left. But Mrs. Webster zeroed in on her son with an expression on her face that said something was wrong.

"You don't look well, Austin. Are you sure you're okay after everything that happened today?"

Everything that happened today? Austin and Ashley traded

a glance. On top of what their mom already knew, make that one volcanic eruption, one chase of a look-alike vandal through an ash desert, a canoe trip across a doomed mountain lake, and a near landing on one of Io's lava superpimples.

All before bedtime.

"I'm doing…" He paused before he said "okay," which was his mistake. That brought the mom-radar to life, and his mother swooped in to place a palm against his forehead.

"Just okay? You feel hot. I think you have a fever. I'll bet you picked up a virus somewhere."

"Maybe. I'm just really tired." Austin did a quick system check. *Both eyes working again? Check. Ears in place? Yep. Ten fingers wiggling? Go.* But to tell the truth, all of a sudden he didn't feel that hot. Or actually, he did—hot *and* cold. Sweats and shivers at the same time. And now his head throbbed and his throat felt like it had been rubbed with sandpaper. This was not good.

"I think you need to go to bed right now." She turned him around and pointed him toward his bed. "And I don't know if you're going to be going to school tomorrow."

"Mom." Ashley reminded her, and their mother clapped a hand to her own cheek.

"Oh, that's right. I'm sorry. Well, we'll see how you feel by tomorrow afternoon, when we have to go meet with the principal. And you know what? I'm sure we'll be able to clear everything up. But right now you need to get a good night's sleep."

"I feel like I could sleep for the next twenty-four hours." Austin shuffled toward his bed while his sister and mom cleared out. His teeth chattered, his eyeballs ached, and he was ready to dive under the covers.

He remembered his mom saying something about praying for him, but then his head fogged up. The last thing he saw before his mom shut the door was his sister standing in the hallway with her arms crossed and one of those "nevah give up" looks on her face.

Like she had a plan, which was a dangerous thing.

Ashley hunched over her desk and added everything up in her head. She did some of her best thinking later at night, when everything was quiet. She didn't like the way things had worked out so far, so she wrote the facts out on a scratch pad to try to make more sense of them.

1. Somebody else is inside the Internet, spying on us. The more she replayed the day's happenings in her head, the more certain she was. Back in Pompeii, Austin hadn't been in two places at once. He couldn't have been. And there hadn't been a glitch in the Web site either. No, someone else had been there, watching her and then hiding around a corner, or run-ning ahead—someone who dressed and looked like Austin.

But why? She would come back to that one.

2. Somebody spray-painted the "I Have a Dream" mural and made it look like Austin did it. No matter what Mr. Hayward might think, it definitely hadn't been her brother. That much she knew, even though the real vandal had painted Austin's name. And come to think of it, wasn't that the tip-off? Who would spray-paint his own name on something and expect to get away with it? She wrote that down to ask at the meeting tomorrow, in case Dad and Mom let her come.

3. Austin zapped the vandal into the Internet, but that person didn't seem lost. Not by the look of his tracks, anyway—they went directly to the link, and the mystery person always seemed to stay just ahead of Ashley and Austin. Assuming the tracks belonged to the mystery person, that is. Ashley wasn't sure he knew how to get back out to the real world, but that was another story, because he sure seemed at home on the Web. The main thing was to find him—wherever he was—and clear Austin's name. Because by now Ashley was pretty sure there was more to it than the vandalism.

Okay, so it would take more noodling and investigating to get to the bottom of things. On the other hand, the snack she was eating tasted like pencil shavings. Ashley looked at what she was holding in her hand. *Oh gross.* She tossed the rest of the mutilated pencil into her trash bucket and picked up a pen instead, anxious to come up with a plan.

She penned out her two main options:

1. Do nothing and watch Austin get into total trouble for something he didn't do. But that wasn't right. Besides, he'd been trying to help her when all the trouble first started. The way Ashley looked at it, she'd gotten him into this mess, and she was going to help him get out. This was a matter of her honor.

2. Track down the real bad guy and bring him back before three tomorrow afternoon, when the principal wants to see Austin. That would be the best plan of action. Problem was, Austin looked like he was out of commission in more ways than one—sick and suspended. So it was up to her and Jessi.

Which gave Ashley an idea. If she could get onto the Internet herself, she might be able to pull it off. After all, real time wasn't the same as time online. It wouldn't take long. In fact, if she didn't have art class first thing tomorrow morning…

Art class? Actually, that gave her an even better idea. She put her ear to the door, though, to be sure no one was up and out in the hallway, before she tiptoed over to her brother's room.

Snoring. Good. Austin wouldn't miss his laptop or the digital camera—not until he woke up, and that could be a long time after she had left for class tomorrow morning.

Ashley hurried back to work on the rest of her plan.

CHAPTER 10

Art Class to the Rescue

A brilliant plan. Daring. Simple. Foolproof.

At least Ashley thought so—and she did say so herself.

"Are you sure it's going to work?" Jessi didn't sound quite as certain as she trotted along beside Ashley to school the next morning, earlier than usual.

"Oh ye of little faith." Ashley did her best to sound sure of herself, more sure than she felt.

"Well, it'd better be good, since you dragged me out of bed so early." Jessi rubbed her eyes. "And what about your brother? He's going to be hopping mad when he sees you took his laptop without asking."

"What was I supposed to do? He's probably going to be sleeping until noon. Boys are like that when they're sick. You didn't want me to wake him up, did you?"

Jessi laughed, but Ashley could tell by her face that she still wasn't convinced.

"Relax." Ashley tried her best to smooth things over. "Austin's not going to mind. I left him a note. And besides, if he gets up and needs to use a computer, he can always use mine."

"Oh, he'll love that." Jessi grinned, and Ashley knew she was thinking of the old hand-me-down brick with a keyboard that Ashley used to write papers and send e-mail. Cool so far. But Jessi didn't know about the e-mail Ashley and Austin had received that morning, before anyone else could check. Did Jessi need to know? Nah.

On second thought, Ashley needed to tell somebody. If nothing else, she wanted to make sure she had understood what the message said.

"Jess?" Jessi was probably the wrong person to ask this kind of thing, but Ashley was more or less stuck.

"Huh?" Jessi could sound halfway intelligent if she wanted to. It's just that maybe she didn't want to.

"I'm going to show you an e-mail, and I want you to tell me what you think it means, okay?"

Jessi shrugged. "Sure. No problem."

Ashley pulled the rumpled printout from her jeans pocket and flattened it out a bit before showing it to her aunt.

Jessi squinted as she read. " 'Heretofore'… Is that really a word?"

"Just read it."

"Okay. 'Heretofore any unauthorized attempts to access

the Internet will be met with immediate corrective action, including but not limited to reprogramming and reconfiguring your unauthorized digital representation as deemed necessary and appropriate by my client. Sincerely, Dewey, Cheettim, and Howe, attorneys-at-law representing the Normal Council on Civil Correctness.'"

Jessi started to laugh and then looked over at Ashley.

"This isn't for real, is it? Tell me you made this up. Especially the stuff about—"

"I am not making this up."

"No way."

"Way."

Jessi looked down at the paper and then back up at Ashley. "In other words, don't go on the Internet or you're toast?"

"Not bad. You actually got through some of that lawyer-speak."

"See? I'm not as much of a blonde as you think."

"I never said you were a blonde." She paused and took back the paper. "Well, except for your hair."

"So does this change your plan for this morning?"

"Not for a second. They're not going to know what hit 'em."

Jessi smiled. "Go, Ashley."

Five minutes later Jessi and Ashley had set up Austin's laptop in the ceramics section of the Chiddix Junior High art room, out of sight but warmed up and ready for the rest of the class to show up. Dawn Madison was first to arrive, a good hour before class and about sixty-two minutes before Mr. Freedlander, the art teacher, would come dashing into the room.

"I brought a piece of rope, just in case." Dawn waved a coil of clothesline.

"In case what?" Ashley looked it over.

"Well, to capture the bad guy!"

Oh.

By that time Eric and Moriah and Sarah T. arrived, plus a few others. Sarah had brought a pile of twelve bright green AbNormal Fitness Center T-shirts, since her dad owned the center. "And we're all going to be on the same team, right?"

"I hope this is important." Eric announced to the gathering crowd. "You know I don't usually get up this early."

"Eric!" Ross Everson rolled his eyes. "Try thinking about somebody other than yourself for a change."

"What are you talking about?" Eric wasn't backing down.

"Hold on." Ashley squeezed in between Ross and Eric and raised her hands for peace. "I'm just glad you're all here."

She looked around and counted…nine, ten, eleven…

"Who's missing?" she asked.

The door slammed and Romaine Foster tripped in with a "Sorry I'm late." *Now* everyone was here.

"Thanks for coming in before class." Ashley looked around the room at the group of art students. A dozen of the goofiest, most creative kids in the school ought to be able to find the Austin look-alike, right? Well, if *they* couldn't…

"I know I didn't tell you anything much last night on IM," Ashley began, "and I'm sorry about that. But you know what happened to Austin yesterday."

Word travels fast, right? Everybody nodded as Ashley went on.

"And you all know he didn't do it, which is why we're here, right?"

"Are you sure he didn't—" Eric began to ask, but Dawn elbowed him in the side.

"Of course he didn't do it, Eric," Dawn told him. "Don't ask silly questions."

Eric rubbed his side and mumbled but didn't say anything else.

"It's a fair question, Eric." Ashley checked her watch. "But I don't have time to explain much right now. Class is starting in about fifty-nine minutes, and we have until then to catch the real troublemaker. You just have to take my word for it, and anyway, you know Austin wouldn't do that kind of thing."

"So what do we do about it?" Ross wanted to know. "What can we do in an hour?"

Ashley smiled at the perfect lead-in question and gave them the two-minute briefing. What to do. How to do it. When to do it. By the end of her pep talk, all the kids were either staring at her or giggling.

Ross was looking around the room. "There's a hidden camera somewhere, right? Taping us for a joke? *Candid Camera*?"

Ashley knew that's what he would say.

"The only camera here is the one that's going to take you where we're going. Now, don't forget: I'm going to be keeping track of you all from here, but you have to put on your AbNormal green T-shirts, which we got on the spur of the moment, thanks to Sarah."

Sarah smiled and took a small bow as Ashley went on.

"And you need to find any links where the guy has already been. And when you find him, everybody go to the same place, okay? Dawn has rope. Don't let him get away."

"And he looks like Austin?" Moriah asked in her teeny, high-pitched voice.

"From what we could tell, yeah. Okay, now we're going to go in groups of two, so stick together like you would if you were in downtown Chicago or something. Check out as many sites as you can. Look for spray paint in places it shouldn't be.

The vandal was in volcano sites yesterday, but last I checked this morning, he was in art sites. Perfect for us."

Ross was still snickering, but he pulled on the oversize shirt just like everybody else.

"This is pretty good, Ash. Sure…I'll be on TV. That's what this is, right? My big reality-TV debut?"

"Sort of. Only better."

Jessi took Romaine Foster by the arm while Ashley readied the digital camera. This was how her brother had done it, wasn't it? How hard could it be?

"Jessi and Romaine are first," she told the group.

Jessi smiled and waved as the flash went off. For the next few seconds all Ashley could hear was the tick of the wall clock.

Finally, Eric tiptoed over to the spot where the two girls had been.

"Whoa." His jaw hung open at least as far as everyone else's as he circled the spot.

"It's safe, you guys. Honest. I've been there and back." Ashley put a little more oomph into her voice to sound as sure as she didn't feel. Not that she would send her friends into danger. But now that her plan was happening, it was a little different from just having the great idea last night.

At last Eric turned to face her with a grin.

"All right." He raised his arms. "Go ahead and beam me up."

"You've got to go with somebody." Ashley pointed to another boy. "Get in the picture, Ross."

"Huh?" Ross didn't seem too sure, but Sarah T. sort of pushed him in toward Eric. Good for her.

"All right, smile." Ashley looked through the viewfinder. Eric smiled while Ross looked around with a worried expression, as if he was thinking he might never come back.

"Back in ten?" he asked.

"Don't worry about it," Ashley answered as she snapped their photo. "Time seems different on the Web."

Poof. There went Eric and Ross. Then Sarah T. and Moriah, Dawn and the other Sara, Sara with no *h*. (Her last name was Westfall.) Adam and Anna. Kimmi and Brianne.

And then Ashley went to work in the quiet art room. Mr. Freedlander would be there in less than an hour now, and she knew she'd better have the class back by then—even if they hadn't caught the troublemaker.

Or she'd be in just as much trouble as her brother.

CHAPTER 11

Painting Pickle

RadAd22: testing 1-2-3. this is awesome! just 1 thing, though—

The first instant message popped up on Ashley's (make that Austin's) laptop, along with the audio. That would be Adam, and she'd already set up an IM window for him, plus eleven more for all the others and six view windows to keep track of where the six teams were. Juggling this many people was almost harder than doing a flip on the balance beam!

Got you. She typed back. *See anything yet?*

Adam and Anna had landed inside a site called *www .FamousDutchPainters.org,* which would have...

RadAd22: lotz of windmlls and stuff. very cool...xcept for the spray-painted scribbles all over. plus anna is getting soaked.

Scribbles? Ashley toggled over to the screen and located Adam on the site. There—Anna was bailing water from a canal boat full of holes, and someone had scribbled big, ugly *x*'s and *o*'s across the clouds in the background, like tick-tack-toe.

Definitely not the way a beautiful painting was supposed to look.

Yeah, he's been there, she typed to Anna and Adam before switching over to see what Kimmi and Brianne were doing. *Keep looking.*

Easy for her to say. She wasn't right in the middle of things. But Kimmi and Brianne, who were at *www.OrigamiPlus.org,* weren't doing much better. In fact...

gimmikimmi: whats wrong with this place, ashley? this isnt funny!

Maybe it wasn't funny in person. But anybody who happened to visit the origami Web site to learn how to make Japanese folded paper art would have to giggle as Kimmi ran from left to right, then back again from right to left.

And that wasn't a nice folded-paper crane, was it? The bird had a huge beak and bigger wings than Ashley had ever seen. It looked more like a dinosaur bird, a pterodactyl or something. And Kimmi was only just staying ahead of its snapping beak.

gimmikimmi: get this monster bird away from me!

Ashley took a closer look and noticed Brianne in the other bright green T-shirt in a corner of the screen. She was hiding behind directions for making a cute bear out of folded tissue paper. But as Ashley watched, the cute origami bear started to sniff the air and stretch his folded-paper paws. Brianne quickly crawled away.

Uh-oh. Someone had obviously been messing with this site as much as the last one. Ashley did some quick clicking to find them a way out.

Sorry, you guys, she typed as fast as her fingers would let her. *Step on the link to the Japanese tea gardens. Five feet to your left. That should be safe for now.*

She hoped.

Meanwhile, messages from the other four teams started chiming in:

lettucegirl: ash, did u see all the heads on the statues here have been sawed off?

That would be from Romaine and Jessi. She checked out the site, and sure enough, the two girls were tiptoeing through a world of famous sculptures, now all hacked up. Was anybody else starting to see a pattern here?

bossross101: eric is missing.

Oh great. Already? Ashley switched over to where she had sent the boys, *www.ClassicsInOil.com.* That would be oil as in oil *paintings,* and it looked as if Ross was poking around in a farmhouse, behind the classic painting of the sour-faced farmer and his wife. What was it called? *American Gothic?*

Ashley stopped. Something looked very familiar about the

farmer, at least from where she sat. Of course, Ross was still back in the farmhouse and could see only the back of the guy's head. Then she realized what must have happened, and she groaned. This was not the way it was supposed to work. But then nothing was working the way the Web usually worked—especially not since she'd sent the art class into the Internet. What was going on here?

Try walking around to the front of the farmer with the pitch-fork, she typed to Ross, and then waited a moment. Pretty soon she got a scream-message back as Ross tried to shake the farmer's shoulders.

bossross101: aaaaagh! eric turned in2 a farmer! how do i unfreeze him?

Don't move. I have to check on the others, but I'll get right back to you.

By this time the IM chimes were binging and bonging nonstop.

Brrriiing!

SaraNoH: Excuse me, Ashley, but Dawn and I are wondering if the Internet is supposed to be like this.

Sara was the only one in the group whose computer was set up so she could write regular sentences and spell everything spelling-bee correct in her IM, even saying "please" and "excuse me." But Ashley couldn't believe her eyes when she toggled over to their site.

"Oh my." She could make out where Sara and Dawn stood only when one of the girls moved a hand to try to wipe the black and gold paint out of her eyes. Whatever Ashley was looking at, it had once been a painting in a fancy museum.

SaraNoH: I hope we didn't ruin it. But as soon as we stepped in here, the sky started oozing.

Not good. The only team Ashley hadn't heard from was—

MoreMoriah: this is 2 weird, ash. how do we get out? i wanna help ur brother, but...

Ashley was afraid to guess what had happened to Moriah and Sarah T., the team she'd sent to look through *www .cubists.com*. With their luck...

But she had to see, so she clicked to the site that showed abstract art, art by artists who used squares and triangles and other shapes in their paintings to make weird versions of reality.

Sure enough.

TotallySarah99: no sign of austin or ur vandal. how r we supposed to c anything here anyway?

Good question. Sarah stood looking straight ahead, hands where her hips would have been. Only it was kind of hard to tell, considering her triangle-shaped body and cube head. Good thing she could still talk. And good thing Sarah couldn't see Moriah—yet.

"Don't worry, you guys." Ashley did her best to sound

cool. "I'll get you out of there right away. Looks like there might be a little problem with the site's program."

MoreMoriah: LITTLE problem? did you say LITTLE? WHAT HAPPENED TO MY EAR? IT'S GONE!

Okay, so that really wasn't good. Ashley was getting ready to bail on the search for the Austin look-alike and rescue her teams when she heard the door squeak open. Mr. Freedlander hadn't come early, had he?

CHAPTER 12

Supposed to Be Mad

"There you are." Austin's voice sounded weak and wheezy, as if he still wasn't quiet awake. His hair stood up in a dozen different directions, and his eyes opened only halfway into puffy slits. Plus his pajama top was stuffed inside his pants, and there was a tissue hanging out of his sleeve.

"Whoa." Ashley finally got her heart put back where it belonged. "You look like death warmed over."

"Thanks," he croaked. "That's about how I feel."

For a minute he looked as if he was going to topple over; then he caught himself and closed the door behind him.

"I can explain—" Ashley started, but he just held up his hand.

"Don't. I know what you're doing."

"You do?"

He nodded. "I woke up right after you left, checked your

e-mail. I threw on some clothes and ran down here as soon as I saw what they were saying."

"But aren't you supposed to be suspended…and home sick in bed, besides?"

"Nobody saw me come here." He coughed into his sleeve. "And I feel great."

"I don't believe you for a second."

"Well, I couldn't let you crash and burn. Did you really send all twelve of the kids in your art class onto the Web?"

She nodded. "I thought it would be the fastest way to round up Graffiti Guy and clear your name. I'm…"

She was going to say "I'm sorry," but the words stuck in her throat. Austin surprised her, though. Maybe the cough syrup Mom had given him was slowing him down, but he wasn't blowing steam out of his ears the way she thought he would be.

"Too late now." He scooted in to take over the laptop's keyboard. "You probably overloaded the connection. Just don't do it again."

"But we still have to find that vandal!" She knew they still had a chance. "He's been to a lot of the sites my classmates are on."

He clicked around for a minute or two, mumbling stuff like "hmm" and "oh yeah."

"Can you tell what's going on?" she asked at last. "What's with all the wild programming?"

"Viruses and worms."

"Huh?"

"Viruses and worms. Nasty little programs that people make to slip into and mess up other people's computer files and programs—and Web sites, too. Sometimes hackers even sneak in by asking people for their passwords, copying them, and faking their way right in the front door of a site. Doing that, they can cover a lot of ground in no time."

Austin hit a few more keys as he went on.

"I'd guess the guy with the spray can is a computer hacker too. Not bad, but his work is a little messy."

"Messy. You saw—"

"Yeah. He's made it pretty random. In some sites, your friends are digitized right into the new look. In others, they get hit in the face by the mess instead."

"Not good."

Austin nodded. "Looks like he's all over the Internet, laying down viruses and worms to destroy any site we go onto, any place we follow him."

"Sort of like land mines."

"Yeah. And right now he's linking to other art sites." He pointed to a list of sites dropping down on one side of his screen. "See? On my Linkz Tracker, he's already been to *www-dot-StreetArt-dot-com*. That links to *www-dot-HandwritingOnTheWall-dot-com,* which links to, well, a bunch of other places."

"He's moving fast."

"They'll never catch up with him. And it's going to take me awhile to get them out."

"Oh." At least she had tried. Ashley stared at the site where Ross was trying to get Eric the farmer's attention. A message was going up on the wall of the farmhouse.

Austin was here.

"It looks like that guy's still trying to make it look like you're the one ruining things! Even online." Ashley was hopping mad now. Wasn't there something she could do?

"Whatever he's doing, he's leaving those viruses and worms all over the place behind him. I have a virus program that can sweep them all up and bring them back to my computer, but it's going to take some time to make it work."

Everything took time. And that's the one thing her brother didn't have.

"Yeah, but what if…" She noodled an idea for a second. "What if you could drop me into the Web right ahead of him, or right on top of him? Wouldn't that work?"

Austin closed his eyes for an instant and frowned.

"Kind of risky, but maybe. Chances are we'd drop you into a link he wasn't going to."

"Or maybe not. Maybe I'd get there just in time."

"And then what? What if you *do* get to a site before him?"

Ashley tried not to think about that part.

"I'll figure something out—and probably get back in time for class too. Come on, Austin. You've got to let me try. Besides, you need to get all the kids back here before Mr. Freedlander comes. And you've got to get home before anybody sees you here too. You're still sick and suspended, remember?"

"I keep forgetting." He coughed again.

"Just let me try."

"I don't know why I let you talk me into these things. I was supposed to be mad at you for taking my laptop and for messing everything up even more."

"Yeah, but I'm sincere."

"You're also nuts." But he was already adjusting a few settings on his computer. He picked up the camera and aimed. "Hold still before I change my mind."

CHAPTER 13

WebyLonians

Say good-bye to the ruined art Web sites. Ashley found herself in a high-ceilinged room bigger even than the gym back home at Chiddix Junior High, with glittering marble floors and red curtains hung along three walls. Hundreds and hundreds of people, all dressed in fancy robes and dresses and propped up on fat cushions, were whooping it up at table after table piled high with plates of dates and pomegranates, breads, and some kind of rice dish with red meat. An army of servants marched jugs in on their shoulders to refill goblets; others brought in more bowls of food.

Ashley stood off to the side, wishing she could hide behind a curtain and wondering exactly where she had landed. She looked for a scrolling text, knee-high words moving across the "screen" of the Web site that might tell her what was going on. Or maybe a pull-down menu, or some links. Something. Anything.

She jumped when one of the diners noticed her.

"Internaut!" he bellowed, motioning for her to join his group of men and their wives. Obviously he'd seen someone like her before. "You'll have dinner with us. Belshazzar would approve."

"Belshazzar?" The name didn't ring any bells.

"The Webylonian king, of course." He frowned. "I thought all internauts would know."

"Sorry." Ashley held up her hand. "Actually, I'm just passing through."

And I'm searching for my link out of here, she thought. It looked as though she'd missed the hacker.

But the guy at the table wasn't taking no for an answer.

"I insist." He bumped the woman at his side to make a place for Ashley. She sighed and shuffled up to the table just as one of the waiters arrived with his jug.

"Some ID, miss? You look like you're under twenty-one."

"N-no thanks," Ashley stuttered when she figured out why he was asking. "Maybe a glass of water, please?"

The waiter raised his eyebrows as if no one had ever asked for that before, but he bowed and left the room. In his place, other waiters brought in piles of grapes and figs and bowls of steaming stuff that reminded her of avocado dip.

And avocado dip made her break out all over. She was searching for a way out when someone started playing footsie with her under the low table. *Excuse me?* The people around her laughed at a joke, seeming not to notice. But when something tickled her ankle again, she had to look.

Oh. Finally she'd found this site's scrolling text, and the words were tickling her ankles as they brushed past. She watched them move by under the table.

Daniel 5:1... King Belshazzar gave a great banquet for a thousand of his nobles and drank wine with them.

Oh, that *Belshazzar.* Now Ashley remembered him—sort of. Belshazzar was in the Bible. Only she wasn't quite sure which Bible story this Web site was showing her. Anyway, if Graffiti Guy didn't show up in two minutes, she was calling Austin for help. Meantime, she glanced down at the words again.

Daniel 5:3... So they brought in the gold goblets that had been taken from the temple of God in Jerusalem, and the king and his nobles, his wives and his concubines drank from them.

That didn't sound right to Ashley. They shouldn't have been using temple stuff for their dinnerware, for sure.

"Lose your sandals, Miss Internaut?" It was a wonder the man next to her didn't choke from stuffing his face with grapes. His cheeks bulged like a chipmunk's as he chewed and talked.

"No." She nibbled on a couple of the grapes herself as the waiter brought her water. She wondered if she should have asked for a paper cup as she kept an eye on the story scrolling past her feet.

Daniel 5:4… They praised the gods of gold and silver, of bronze, iron, wood and stone.

Okay, time to leave. This was getting too weird. Was Austin keeping track of all this? But when she saw the next verse, Ashley finally realized which story this Web site was probably programmed to tell.

Daniel 5:5… Suddenly the fingers of a human hand appeared and wrote on the plaster of the wall, near the lampstand in the royal palace. The king watched the hand as it wrote.

So did everyone else, and the clinking of goblets stopped as the crowd hushed. This graffiti looked like squiggly Hebrew writing, and obviously Ashley couldn't read what it said.

At least she could understand the instant message that popped up right next to the scrolling text under the table.

Webster1: hey ashley do u see what i see?

It was about time for her brother to pop in. The handwriting on the wall had creeped her out, just as it had the man in the purple robe at the head of all the tables.

Daniel 5:6… His face turned pale and he was so frightened that his knees knocked together and his legs gave way.

A couple men near him rushed to make sure he wasn't hurt.

"My king!" one of them shouted. "It's just a…"

Just a what? The rescuer couldn't finish what he was saying; he didn't know what it was either. Everyone looked back at the wall, but by that time the hand had disappeared.

What's more, a new message had appeared next to the first one. But this one was written in spray paint! And it said, *Austin was here.*

"Oh brother." Ashley tried to hide her eyes with her hand. Graffiti Guy had finally caught up with her. Only where was he?

Webster1: Ashley?

"I saw it, Austin," she whispered back. "How about getting me out—"

Webster1: speak a little louder would u? u r coming in kinda fuzzy…hard 2 read.

"I SAID…" When she spoke straight at her brother's IM, everyone at her table turned to stare at her. *Whoopsie.*

"It's the internaut's doing!" One of the ladies pointed at Ashley. "She brought the messages."

"No, hold it. Wait a minute." Ashley shook her head. "I don't do floating hands. I don't do spray paint either."

She looked down at the scrolling story text, but it had paused. Maybe that's as far as it went. But another IM came bouncing by.

Webster1: ur link is still good. stay put at www.DanielStory .com *4 now. looks 2 me like the mystery guy is close by.*

Well, she could have told Austin that. But right now Ashley had to worry about a room full of suspicious Webylonians, all staring right at her.

CHAPTER 14

Oss-tin

"Don't touch it!" One of the king's bodyguards placed himself between the crowd and the writing on the wall. Ashley wiggled away from the guard who had pulled her from the table, and she stood there with her arms crossed and her face steaming. Come to think of it, she really didn't feel that well. Maybe Austin had given her his flu bug, or whatever virus he had. *Thanks a lot, bro.*

"I wasn't going to hurt anything, okay?" She couldn't believe this. "I was just trying to read it for you."

"See?" An older, bearded fellow shook a crooked finger at her. "She *was* responsible."

"Oh man." Ashley shook her head again as it started to throb. "I don't know what makes you think that. But listen, let me just say it one more time. I didn't have anything to do with this, and I don't know what it says. The first part, I mean."

And neither did the team of old guys the king called in to

try to read the writing. Astrologers and court wizards—anybody off the streets of Babylon who claimed to be able to read fortunes and tell the future was free to try.

But all they did was blame Ashley, until the guards brought in someone new. The hocus-pocus crew stepped back and gave the newcomer icy stares. If looks could chill...

"Are you Daniel?" the king asked the tall, dark-haired man. Someone had thrown a long silk robe over him, but it didn't quite cover up his buff arms or his bare feet. "One of the exiles my father the king brought from Judah?"

When the man nodded, the king went on about how his men couldn't read the handwritten message, but his wife had told him Daniel might help. And if Daniel could figure it out, there was a promotion in it for him: from slave to third in command.

The crowd made a hubbub at the offer, but Daniel acted as if he didn't care.

"You can keep the gifts and promote somebody else," he told the king, looking him straight in the eye. "Even so, I'll read it for you and tell you what it means."

The crowd parted to make way for Daniel, and Ashley followed the tall Hebrew to the wall.

"Uh, excuse me, Mr. Daniel?" She wasn't quite sure how to tell him. "You don't have to worry about the spray-painted writing over to the side. That's not part of your story."

He stopped.

"It's just…" Ashley lowered her voice, but her tongue tripped over the words. "It's not supposed to be there. It's someone from the Outside trying to make Austin look bad."

"There! I heard that!" The same old guy who had accused her before now pointed at her again. "She prays to her deity again, this Oss-tin. I say we hold her for more study."

"You can't hold me," Ashley sighed. "I'm not part of this site."

Well, that sounded good to her. She turned back to Daniel. "And that's my brother *Austin* we're talking about. We keep in touch with IM."

"IM." Daniel looked at her with squinted eyes. "I'm not going to ask you what that means. I already have enough puzzles on my hands."

He turned back to the wall and traced the strange letters with his hand. He paused for a moment, closing his eyes, and his lips moved silently. And when he opened his eyes again a moment later, he read the words the way Ashley might have read the back of a box of Corn Flakes.

"*Mene, mene, tekel, parsin,*'" he read, moving his finger from one word to the next. "That means, 'God has numbered the days of your reign and brought it to an end.'"

All that in four little words? The crowd around the king puffed up their chests and looked about ready to strangle

Daniel. And they probably would have if the king hadn't raised his shaking hand.

"Go on." The king barely squeaked out the words. "Let him speak."

Daniel went on with the translation. "*Tekel* means you have been weighed on the scales and found wanting."

Another gasp from the crowd. Who spoke to the king like this and got away with it?

"And finally," said Daniel, "it says that…*Austin was here.*"

Oh no. Ashley groaned.

"It's the god of Oss-tin again!" screamed the old wizard, hopping on one foot and pointing once more at Ashley. "She brings his trouble with her!"

That was enough for Ashley.

"Would you guys cool it with the Oss-tin stuff?" She planted her feet as they closed in around her. "I already told you he's not here, and he hasn't been here, no matter what the graffiti says. Sorry, Daniel. It's a big mix-up."

"But Oss-tin!" The wizard was going to be disappointed when he finally figured it out. *If* he ever did.

"Listen," she said. "I don't know how else to explain it to you. Austin is probably still back home in the art room, even though he ought to be home in bed. He's got some kind of virus."

As soon as the V-word slipped from her mouth, Ashley

could have bitten her tongue. She should have known better. A couple women screamed, and the magicians backed away from her, hands in the air, eyes bugged out. Several mumbled some words, and one of them threw a handful of chalk dust in her face.

"No! Not that kind of virus!" she tried to tell them. But by that time a team of a dozen little men had crashed in through the windows.

"Nobody move!" cried one of them. "We're your virus protection program."

Like the rest of the Virus Patrol team, he wore bright white Mr. Clean–style coveralls, bright white tennis shoes, and a bright white helmet with vents in the sides where his pointy little Mr. Spock–like ears stuck out. A big red V on his chest showed the world he was on the Virus Patrol team.

"That's great, but—" But the leader of the virus squad wasn't taking Ashley's no for an answer. He tripped over the nearest pillow and hoisted himself onto the low table. Of course, the knee-high table was taller than he was, but that didn't seem to slow him down. Neither did the tank on his back, and he pulled its nozzle out and pointed it into the air.

"Just stay still," he commanded. "And don't argue. All we do is spray for viruses and worms. Give us ten minutes to sweep it all up, and we're out of here."

"But it's the internaut!" The wizard pointed at Ashley. "We had no trouble until she came. Sweep *her* up, why don't you?"

Two members of the Virus Patrol glanced at each other for a second and then shrugged. They didn't seem bothered by the wizard's concern.

"Wait a minute." Ashley wasn't going to let that comment go. Some of the virus-busters had already begun spraying down the walls and curtains with clear disinfectant, but two or three turned aside to circle around her. "I'm not the virus. They're confused."

Confused or not, this whole Webylonian adventure was spinning out of control, and Ashley still had no clue where the vandal had gone.

"Get that stuff out of my face!" She tried to hold off the spray, which smelled like a cross between watermelon juice and mild bleach—a bad air freshener, for sure. "Aussss-tin!"

She knew the Internet characters would go nuts when they heard that name again. But Austin needed to get her out of there, and she had no idea why he had let her stay this long. The only other thing Ashley could think to do was to dive under the dinner table as the crowd screamed.

CHAPTER 15

Luther Link

What I don't do for my brother... Ashley crawled on all fours under the table, bumping her head in the dark and wondering what kinds of links she might come across. She noticed one for *Old Testament Commentaries on Daniel* and another for *Top Ten Daniel Sites.* She had to shiver as she brushed against still another link, which took her...where?

She blinked as the table and palace faded away. All of a sudden, it seemed a lot colder.

Colder and windier, like a drizzly October day in *www .MartinLuthersWorld.com.* At least that's what it said in tiny, old-fashioned letters along the bottom edge of the site, right next to a man's worn leather shoes. The shoes were connected to a pair of stubby legs standing next to a big wooden door.

She looked up at the man, who was dressed like a priest in a dark brown robe.

"Excuse me." Ashley tried to smile in spite of her chattering teeth. "I was just in Belshazzar's dining room. Not that this isn't a nice place, but…"

She looked around at the muddy street and the tall stone cathedral towering over it. Europe, she guessed. Germany, probably.

"I think I'm lost," she admitted.

The man smiled down at her with a sparkle in his eyes and held out a thick hand to help her up.

"I'm Luther," he told her. "Dr. Martin Luther. And I take it you haven't been sent here to debate my ideas."

As she scrambled to her feet, Ashley was afraid she was looking at him with a blank expression on her face, though she didn't mean to. She just wasn't sure what he meant.

"Never mind. Here, you're a tall girl." He held out a large sheet of paper. "Help me post this on the door, where everyone will see it."

Ashley began to put together the pieces: *This is* www-dot-MartinLuthersWorld-dot-com, *and the guy calls himself Martin Luther. He's tacking up a paper on the door of this church, and though the writing's in German, the list on it numbers from one to ninety-five.*

Wait—she remembered this from Sunday school. Church history for a thousand, please. What famous event happened on October 31, 1517?

"This is where the Protestant church started, isn't it?" she asked, and he raised his eyebrows.

Bingo! Austin would have been proud of her,

"I suppose—*pound-pound*—an internaut like you—*pound-pound*—would recognize such a thing." He fished around in the pocket of his brown robe to find another small tack. "But that's not what Luther had in mind when he, I mean, when I first decided to put this up."

"Really?"

"I may be only the Internet version of a priest here in Wittenberg, dear girl, but I think Luther would be as surprised as anyone to learn that he founded the Protestant church. At least at first. After all, I'm just putting up a few questions on the town bulletin board, wondering if there's anyone else who cares to discuss what I've come to believe."

"Like…?"

He looked at her carefully, as if trying to decide whether she'd understand his theology. At last he shrugged.

"For example, number one, right here." He planted his finger on the first point and read, " 'When our Lord and Master Jesus Christ said, "Repent," he meant that…Austin was here?' "

Oh no. Not again! Ashley's face went pale. All of a sudden things weren't looking so good again.

"This isn't what I wrote!" Martin Luther ripped the famous

paper from the door and skimmed through it. "All the way through to ninety-five… My words are gone. It's got to be a virus! But what kind of programmer would have done this to me?"

Ashley swallowed hard, though she knew it wasn't her fault.

"Do you know who this Austin might be?" he asked.

"Yes…but I need to explain."

But would he believe her? He looked at her almost the same way the wizard had, back at the last site: She's trouble, this one!

Just then, an IM popped up at their feet.

Webster1: yo ashley ur doing great! u didn't know u were going 2 meet the net version of the famous martin luther did u?

"Never mind that," she answered back. "Where have you been all this time? They thought everything was all my fault at the last site, and now…"

Martin Luther looked at her with a wrinkled brow.

"Pardon me," he asked, "but do you always talk to yourself like that?"

She pointed out the IM words and explained.

"It's my brother, Austin—Webster1. He's talking to me from back home."

"Austin, you say?" Now he was interested. Really interested.

"No. I mean, yes, that's his name. But he didn't do anything to your paper. Honest. There's a hacker on this site who's pretending that he's my brother. That's why I'm here; to try and find him."

Webster1: ask him if u can zip ahead 4 years to another luther site. i think that's where our guy is headed. 4 years. hit the time-line to 1521.

That was easy enough for him to say. Ashley rushed around the edges of the cathedral, looking for the right link.

Webster1: go left, then 10 steps. i think i see something there.

She skipped over links to *Lutheran Life Insurance* and *Camp Lutherwood,* stopping where she thought Austin had said to.

Webster1: right there! where it says Diet of Worms.

Whoa! What?

"I don't think so, Austin. What do worms have to do with Martin Luther? And I'm sure not going on *that* kind of diet."

Webster1: ROFL! worms is the name of the city, and diet is another name for council. get it?

Why hadn't he said so in the first place? Ashley looked over her shoulder at the feisty Martin Luther, still shaking his head over his ruined paper, before she dipped her toe into the new link.

CHAPTER 16

Wormy Diet

Of course, four years later inside the Internet felt like nothing. But Ashley had to keep reminding herself where she was: *www.Diet-of-Worms.org.*

That was a funny name for a very unfunny place. A large room held a group of serious old men sitting behind a big wooden table, all staring at Martin Luther, who stood in front of them. A younger guy came lumbering in with armloads of books and unloaded them all on the table in front of the council—the diet.

"Hi, Dr. Luther!" Ashley came up behind him and whispered her hello. "How have you been doing?"

"Ah, the young internaut with the hacker brother." This time he didn't smile; he just raised his eyebrows. "I remember you from the other site."

Ashley wondered what kind of programming had pulled

the same Martin Luther from *www.MartinLuthersWorld.com* to this site.

"As for how am I doing," he went on. "I would have supposed you already knew. But then, you're probably not clever enough to have caused all the damage."

"What damage?" Ashley didn't take the put-down personally.

Dr. Luther raised his eyes and looked up at the ceiling, which had been spray-painted with ugly drawings of cats and weird squiggly lettering—and Austin's name all over the place.

"All the pages of my old site are shutting down," he whispered back. "One by one. The link to this site was my last hope, and I'm surprised it worked."

Ashley took it all in. The damage seemed to be getting worse all the time.

"I'm really sorry. We're trying to stop the person who's doing this."

He bit his lip and looked straight at her.

"I think I believe you. Yes…perhaps I do."

Well, that was a step in the right direction. But they still had the diet to deal with. And on an infected site like this, they might crash at any time.

As in, *fffft!*—this Web site is down, dead, done. Ashley didn't want to think too much about what would happen to her if she was still inside it when that happened.

"Silence!" The sternest of the stern men clapped his hands and looked over his spectacles at them. Floating in front of his place at the table was a small name tag with lettering in a heavy, old-fashioned script: *Dr. Johann Eck.* He kind of flickered, as did the rest of the site, like the light from a weak flashlight.

Dr. Eck pointed a bony finger at Ashley.

"What is this internaut doing here?"

"She is an acquaintance of mine," answered Luther, "and says she has nothing to do with the hacker attacks. I have reason to believe her sincerity."

"Ha! Someone else who's sincere. We'll see." He shuffled a parchment. "In any case, I have two questions for you, *Dr.* Luther." He spit out the "doctor" part as if it was hard for him to say. "First, you will tell the diet whether you are in fact the author of the stacks of books sitting here."

Luther took his time thumbing through the stacks before nodding and telling them he was.

"Very well." Dr. Eck went on. "Then I ask you whether you will now admit you were wrong and retract every word. Take it all back."

"He's not going to do that," Ashley blurted out and then wished she hadn't. She clapped a hand to her lips and whispered a quick "Sorry," but Eck pointed straight at her.

"That will be the last outburst, Internaut, or I'll have you reprogrammed and put out of this room."

Can he do that?

Martin Luther winked at her and launched into a theological discussion about how grace and faith are the only way to heaven. "Giving extra offerings won't do it," he said, "and—"

"No, no, no!" Johann Eck's face turned red. "I asked a simple yes or no question. I want a simple yes or no answer!"

This time Luther raised an eyebrow and stroked his chin before he answered.

"All right, then. You want me to take it back? Well, unless you can show me from Scripture where I've made mistakes, I cannot do that. There's no way I can take anything back. It would be too dangerous to go against my conscience. And that's where I stand. God help me if I'm wrong."

Dr. Eck slammed his fist down on the table and swept Luther's books to the floor.

"You're going to regret this, Luther! Hackers and worms are nothing compared to the trouble you're asking for."

Well, maybe so. But Dr. Eck hadn't seen the worm that now inched its way across the floor, behind his chair. Worm? This monster was more like a gator without legs.

"Uh, Dr. Eck, sir?" Ashley tried to get his attention, but he just held up his hand.

"I told you, not a word from you!"

"But—"

This time Austin's timing was better than before, and his IM dropped right onto the table where Martin Luther's books had been. Right where everyone could see it.

Webster1: HEY ASHLEY! LOOK BEHIND YOU!

Good advice. The first worm had been joined by three more, each leaving a slime trail behind it and moving faster than one would think a worm could move.

"Quickly," shouted Luther. "You'd better leave!"

And he pushed her toward the nearest link.

CHAPTER 17

Virus Patrol

Austin blinked his eyes and did his best to stay awake. Even with all the excitement, he couldn't keep from yawning on his spot on the couch back home. Maybe it was the cough syrup. At least his fever was down. And at least he'd made it safely home with his laptop, without having to power it all the way down.

"Where is that turkey?" He clicked on the page again, but Graffiti Guy always kept one step ahead. He'd never seen anyone move so quickly, even on the Web. The Virus Patrol said he was one place, and—*bam!*—he was on to the next.

A quick check of his watch showed Austin it was 8:00 a.m. Thank goodness he didn't have to worry anymore about the kids from his sister's art class. He giggled at the memory of how serious they'd looked when he made them all hold up their right hands and promise not to tell what they'd seen that morning inside the Internet.

"Hey, no problem," Ross had answered. "Who's going to believe our psycho story, anyway?"

Good boy, Ross. But there wasn't time to think more about that now. Austin had his hands full sending his Virus Patrol program into the damaged sites, cleaning up the viruses and worms littered around the Internet like candy wrappers in a school lunchroom. Keeping track of Ashley only made things trickier.

u r doing great, sister, he typed into his IM window, though he wasn't sure she was getting all his messages. *sorry u r going to be late for class. but don't give up.*

Easy for him to say. He'd had the toughest time catching up to her again after she slipped out of the palace at *www .DanielStory.com.* And now she had slipped to another link, right behind where his virus detector told him the hacker had gone. But not before the guy had let loose three of the deadliest worm programs Austin had ever seen.

The poor Diet of Worms site was toast.

So it was probably good Ashley had jumped ship, hyperlinking to somewhere else. But this was getting ridiculous.

Ridiculous didn't quite cover it. Ashley was sure this site was megadisgusting. Probably worse. The guy standing in front of her wasn't helping her opinion any. He was chewing a huge wad of gum with his mouth open and was digging his hand into a coffee can of...

gross,

nasty,

slimy

worms.

"Internet special," he told her, letting the wiggly worms plop back down into the can. "Five pounds of red wigglers delivered next-day air to your doorstep, right here from *www-dot-earthworm-magic-dot-com.* Guaranteed fresh and live or your money back. Just enter your postal code here"—he pointed at a small box floating in the air—"and we'll give you an instant shipping quote. Fish can't resist 'em."

"Well, I sure can." Ashley looked around at the raised beds of virtual sawdust—an Internet worm garden. "No offense, but—"

"No problem; I'll just show you around the site. I'm Everett, by the way, and I'll be your online host for today. Click over there for secrets of composting, a forty-eight-page booklet personalized just for you. Click there for a free worm-words glossary, all you'd ever like to know about our wiggler friends. And over here for the worm forum, where you can chat with folks all over the world about my *favorite* subject: red wigglers!"

"Terrific." Ashley looked to see if Graffiti Guy had been there, but her host was too excited about the site tour.

"Hey, let me tell you about the two best kinds of red worms: *Eisenia foetida* and *Lumbricus rubellus*. Did you know it takes about a thousand wigglers to make one pound?"

"I had no idea."

"That's right." He hiked up his overalls. "And..."

Ashley waited for him to finish his sentence. His mouth moved for a few seconds, but no sound came out.

Then—"pulverized eggshells, coffee grounds, and..."

He acted as if nothing had happened and kept on with his herky-jerky tour, some of his words dropping out here and there.

"Wait a minute." Ashley raised her hand. "Did I miss something? I think you're having audio problems."

"...even manure piles...red worms are very..."

She watched him for a couple minutes, trying to follow the conversation with half the words cut out, until Austin's IM caught up with her at last.

Webster1: just came from the diet of worms. i think our guy is still there. can u go back?

"The Diet of Worms? No way. It was about to shut down, and they're not real happy with me there, either. That Dr. Eck was pretty tough."

"Did somebody say Diet of Worms?" Everett was right on it. "I can...you...right...no extra charge!"

"Huh?" Ashley wasn't sure she wanted to know what he'd said.

"I'll take...as a yes." He took her by the arm. "Follow me."

A minute later she wished she hadn't.

Chapter 18

Worm Gag

"And now, for the million-dollar grand prize…" The dashing host seemed to enjoy soaking up the five blinding spotlights shining in his face. "We're going to see which of these blindfolded celebrity contestants can walk the balance beam over the pit of crocodiles while eating a can of worms, live in front of a worldwide Internet audience. Welcome to *www-dot-PanicFactor-dot-com*! The world's only interactive Internet reality show where *you* choose what happens next, and *you* decide who wins!"

Click-click-click-click…

People from the Outside clicked on the Web celeb they wanted to see. Like the host, the contestants on this site had name tags floating above their heads—a pop singer named Natasha, a sitcom actress named Alison, or a rapper named Qual-e-Tee. All Internet versions of the real celebrities.

Even so, everything looked and sounded real enough,

especially the crocs in the big pool below. Ashley heard a roar of cheers and clapping as the wild-haired host, Brian B. Best, smiled and waved to the ring of Web cams set up all around them. The place reminded her of some kind of Roman stadium, only the contestants wore safety harnesses attached to bungee cords.

Was Austin watching this?

"And here, friends, is the lovely mixture each contestant must finish off as quickly as possible before reaching the other side: a can of juicy red wiggler worms, courtesy of our good friends at *www-dot-earthworm-magic-dot-com*!"

"Finish off," as in *eat*. Swallow. Chow down. Consume.

Everyone in the Web audience went, "Oooo, yuk!" and the Web celebs smiled and clapped. *This* diet of worms made Ashley's stomach turn two and a half flips with a sideways twist. Good thing she wasn't the silly celebrity trying the stunt.

The noise grew louder as the host held up a card in one hand. Then he silenced the crowd with a dramatic wave of the other hand.

"And now, let's read the results. Our first celebrity chosen for the croc-worm challenge is…"

He looked around the room to drag out the excitement.

"Ashley Webster!"

Excuse me? Everyone cheered and pointed at Ashley while she replayed the words in her head to make sure she'd heard them right. The three Web celebs were whispering to one another, looking surprised, as if this wasn't supposed to happen. It wasn't, was it?

"Wait a minute." Ashley held up her hands and backed up a step, but an assistant had already strapped a safety harness around her shoulders and was cinching it tighter. "I'm not in this contest. I'm not even a celebrity! And besides, how do you know my name?"

"This is the Internet, remember?" Brian B. Best smiled for the cameras and pointed to the name tag above her head. "And I'm sure our Web celebs will gladly follow once you set the pace."

"But…"

Ashley was trying to figure a way out of this mess as a second assistant placed the can of wigglers in her hand. At least they didn't try to blindfold her too.

"No thanks, really." Ashley tried to hand it back to the assistants, but they were already leading her to the starting point. Two crocs eyed her and hissed—a nice touch. She wondered if they were programmed to actually eat things and how far her bungee-cord safety line would let her fall from the balance beam if she slipped.

But wait a minute. What was she *doing?*

"FORGET THIS!" She threw the worms down to the hungry crocs, who seemed to appreciate the snack, and tried to undo the harness buckles. No go. "I am not here to be on this show, and even if I was, I wouldn't eat a can full of *disgusting* worms. Not in a million years."

"What about the million bucks?" squeaked the host, coming up beside her. "What about our live, worldwide Internet audience?"

"I don't *care* about the million, and I don't *care* about the live, worldwide Internet audience. Well, I mean, I *care* about them, but not the way you do. This is crazy!"

The host faced her with his arms crossed.

"So you're telling me you want to quit the show, is that it? I have to tell you I'm very disappointed. Our lawyers are going to have to look into this. Folks?"

As the audience applauded, a trio in jet-black suits and red power ties hopped into the arena. They didn't need name tags or an introduction. Their genuine leather briefcases were stenciled with *www.onlinelawyers.com.*

"Do I smell a lawsuit?" One of the lawyers grinned and started to pull some papers out of her briefcase. "Now, how about we all sit down and take a look at these papers. I'm sure we can come to some kind of agreement. Can you spell *breach of contract?*"

"Hold it." Ashley couldn't believe this. "You say I *quit* the show? I never *joined* the show. All I'm here for is to—"

Ka-SPLASH!

Everyone jumped at the sound of the splash. Brian B. Best, the Web celebs, the online lawyers, Ashley...

And everyone looked down in horror to see Austin sitting right in the middle of the shallow croc pool, his digital camera strapped around his neck. Where had he come from?

"Crikey!" He must have realized where he had landed and slowly got to his feet. For now the crocs didn't budge, seeming just as shocked as everybody else. "Looks like I'm a few feet off course this time, mates."

CHAPTER 19

Who's the Rescuer?

Austin didn't have time for a plan when he landed in the croc pool. Neither did Ashley, who yelled, "Grab my legs!" as she flew through the air straight at him, Spiderwoman-style.

With no better ideas, he latched on to her ankles and held on for dear life. So much for coming to help his poor, helpless sister. And he'd thought *he* was going to be the rescuer this time!

Good thing the crocs were too slow-moving and the bungee cord stretched low enough for him to reach Ashley. Seconds later they were both bouncing a few feet above the croc pool. Wasn't there a scene in *Peter Pan* like this?

"Pull up the internauts!" By this time the host had taken charge, and everyone gathered around when they pulled Austin and Ashley to safety.

"Well, this should help our ratings." Brian B. Best looked up at a hit counter in the distance—a gizmo that counted how many people were visiting the site. The numbers were spinning, and he grinned.

"Thanks, Ash." Austin's jeans and pajama shirt were soaked. Well, when you rush to aid a maiden in distress, you don't have time to get totally dressed, right?

"But what are you *doing* here?" Ashley probably wasn't the only one who was wondering that.

"I felt like this was all my fault." He tried to think of a quick way to explain as he looked for the link he wanted. "Because I sent you in the wrong direction before, and then I couldn't get an IM into this site to tell you what was going on."

"Oh. I was wondering."

"Yeah, everything's messed up. The only way I could get word to you was to come here myself."

"Okay, but how are you going to keep track of everything now?"

"If we hurry, I won't need to. I'm pretty sure I know where the hacker is. Just come with me."

"Does that mean you won't be here for a retake of that fantastic landing in the croc pool?" The host looked long faced.

"I wouldn't have called it 'fantastic,' exactly." Austin was ready to jet out of there—back one link and then over one more.

Because there was no telling how long Graffiti Guy would stay in one place.

⌒🖱

"Hi, Dr. Luther. Bye, Dr. Luther!" Ashley waved as they tumbled through two Luther links. But she knew they had no time to stop and chat. If they hurried, her brother had told her, they could zip straight from a diet of worms to the Diet of Worms, from Martin Luther to Martin Luther King Jr. Maybe then they would finally catch up to the hacker.

When everything stopped shifting, they looked around at the new site.

"Wow," Ashley whispered. "Look at all the people."

Austin looked around at the crowd too: thousands and thousands of people, elbow to elbow, a dark sea of faces. And every one of them zeroed in on a man in the distance who was standing behind a podium on a platform in front of the steps of the Lincoln Monument in Washington, D.C. At least it looked like Washington, D.C., with cherry trees and the re-flecting pond and the tall Washington Monument in the dis-tance behind them. If they'd figured this right, she and Austin had linked to *www.MLKingSpeeches.org*.

Right near the bottom of the site, out in front of the crowd, was a bright blue audio controller with sliders for Vol-ume and Start, Fast-Forward, Reverse, and all that. The volume was on full blast, which was fine, and the date counter was set at 8/28/1963.

In other words, August 28, 1963.

"You again!" A large woman sitting in a folding beach chair frowned and batted at Ashley and Austin as if they were flies at a summer picnic. "I already told you once to sit down so everybody can see!"

A few other people echoed her complaint. "Yeah, sit down!"

"Sorry." Ashley caught on quickly. She ducked down and pulled Austin with her. "We're sorry."

"You better decide where you're going, young man." The woman wasn't through with them yet. "Coming and going, going and coming. Why don't you just sit down and listen to the speech? You might learn something."

What did she mean, coming and going? Unless—

Ashley looked at Austin, her eyes wide. He must have understood too.

"He's here!" She looked around.

Or he had been. The *other* Austin. The turkey with the spray paint.

CHAPTER 20

Finding Graffiti Guy

Only problem is, how do we find Graffiti Guy in this ocean of people? Come to think of it, maybe it wouldn't be quite as hard as Austin thought, considering how pale they were compared to most of the folks around them. He scanned the crowd as he listened to the voice over the loudspeakers.

A man was telling everyone he had a dream, a dream of a country where all people really were created equal. Even with the first few words, Martin Luther King Jr.'s rich voice nearly hypnotized Austin. And right away he understood why everyone in the crowd was so focused on this man. His words echoed over their heads, probably carrying all the way to the White House, all across the landscape of *www .MLKingSpeeches.org*. And maybe beyond.

The man's dream? That his own kids would grow up free, not judged for what they looked like, but by their character.

When everyone clapped, Austin couldn't help but join in.

They clapped and clapped, and the speaker mopped his brow as he waited for the crowd to settle. And for a minute Austin forgot about the pesky Internet worms and viruses destroying Web site after Web site. He forgot about being in huge trouble back home, about being sick, and about the strange look-alike kid who had vandalized the mural at the school in Normal. Come to think of it, it had all started with a mural of the same man who now stood in front of these thousands and thousands of people, delivering the speech of the century.

And this man still had a dream that black kids and white kids would one day join hands.

More applause. Austin listened, soaking it all in as the preacher quoted from the Bible, the part about valleys being exalted and rough places being made plain, and the glory of the Lord being revealed, and all flesh seeing it together.

Martin Luther King Jr.'s words reminded Austin of a song he'd heard somewhere before, only he couldn't quite remember where. But that wasn't the end of the dream. One day all of God's children, no matter what their color or race, would stand together and sing the words of that old Negro spiritual: "Free at last! Free at last! Thank God Almighty, we are free at last!"

The crowd had been cheering pretty good up to that point; now they let loose in a roar like Austin had never heard before. Little kids held by their mamas, clapping with chubby hands. Dads standing, hands raised, some of them waving their hats. Old people with white hair, and, nearby, a lady in a wheelchair, shaking her head and saying "amen" over and over again.

Wow. Never mind the rocket-exhaust August heat; Austin couldn't keep the goose bumps from parading up and down the back of his neck. He looked over at Ashley and saw tears streaming down her cheeks. They didn't get to hear stuff like this every day, even online. Austin was thinking of hitting the Replay button on the bright blue audio controller, but then he remembered why they had come in the first place.

Or rather, the hacker reminded him. Because even as Dr. King's last words echoed, a boy down in front reached out and sprayed the controller with black paint, bold as you please.

"Hey!" The woman who had told them to sit down spotted the kid first and pointed. But he just kept right on spraying, covering the control panel with paint so thick Austin couldn't see the buttons or the sliders or the volume controls.

"Come on." Austin grabbed his sister's arm and dove through the crowd, which was easier to say than do. They pressed closer to the guy, who seemed to be having so much fun destroying this Web site that he didn't notice them until they were maybe three or four steps away. And though Austin still wasn't sure what he was going to do when he caught the guy, he knew he would figure that out when the time came.

Like now.

"STOP THAT!" Austin growled as he launched into a flying leap, straight at Graffiti Guy, who stopped painting long enough to look up at him.

Weird as it was tackling someone who looked so much like himself, Austin piled on. When Ashley joined him, they did their best to hold this guy down with all their 163½ combined pounds.

Only thing was, the hacker was either quicker than they had hoped, or stronger. He managed to wiggle to the side, dragging both Ashley and Austin over to the platform. Austin grabbed the boy's belt but came up with only a little black box, smooth and cold.

"That's mine!" The kid tried to grab it back, but Austin slipped it into his back pocket. Meanwhile Dr. King and all the others on the platform jumped out of the way as Austin and his look-alike hit an unmarked link—and dropped through the floor.

Chapter 21

Wrestling Match

Austin hardly had time to catch his breath before they tumbled headfirst into what seemed like a large, empty room. *Whoops.* He wasn't sure what had happened to Ashley or to his digital camera, but he *was* sure what had happened to Graffiti Guy.

"Let…go…of…me," grunted the other boy. But Austin wasn't about to. Not this time. Instead, he locked on and tried to pin the vandal to the floor. He could hear yelling in the background, but he wasn't sure what was being said.

One thing was sure: This wrestling match was creepier than anything he remembered from PE class. It was like staring into a mirror in the morning, only this reflection wasn't smiling back, and he was definitely having a bad hair day.

"Who are you, anyway?" Austin managed to ask. They rolled over once more, knocking over a stack of canvas paintings.

"If I tell you, will you let me go?" Even his voice sounded just like Austin's.

"No promises." Austin held the kid down. "Try me."

"No," he grunted again. "Give me back...the transponder. Then I'll tell you."

Did he mean the thing Austin had in his back pocket?

"Why? What's it do?"

"That's how I get out of here, okay?"

"Out of where?"

"Come on." The guy rolled his eyes. "The Internet. You ever seen an Internet character Outside before?"

Austin suddenly realized what he meant—this guy was digital. "Yeah, once. You made a mess, and I got in trouble for it."

The digital clone—that's what he had to be—grinned. So that black box was an Internet character's ticket to freedom? A way for someone Inside to travel Outside? No wonder he wanted it so badly.

"Worked pretty well, huh?" The clone looked proud. "Just the way Z said it would."

"You mean Mr. Zawistokowski?"

"Whoever. He programmed me. And he's going to make sure you don't get out of here, especially if you don't let me go."

"He wouldn't..."

"You still think he's a nice guy? You have no idea what he wants—what they want. And I guess you're not as smart as I thought you were."

"Well, I caught up with you."

"So you get a gold star. Now let me—"

"All right." Austin figured this guy wouldn't run yet. Not until they made their deal. So he finally looked around to see where he might be.

At first the site reminded him of a pirate's cave, with stolen treasure lining the walls. Only this was a hacker's cave, maybe, with parts of Web sites propped up against the walls, stacked, or floating here and there.

A wrecked Pompeian statue stood next to a mural like the one at Chiddix. Piles of paintings, all damaged, rested against the walls. There was the *Galileo* space probe, with a couple broken antennae. A sputtering fountain from the Webylonian palace. The entry door to Martin Luther's church, hanging crookedly, with the ninety-five theses still attached. And lots more, like so many props from a movie studio in some forgotten warehouse. Only these were stolen bits and pieces of the Internet.

Austin could only shake his head.

"Why? Why did you steal all this stuff, and then ruin it?"

"Ruin it?"

"Spray-paint everything. Hack into all these Web sites. And ruin the Dr. King mural back home."

The clone shrugged. He probably wasn't programmed to feel sorry for anything he'd done. "Z just wanted to get you off the Net any way he could. My job is to make you look bad, like a vandal—or a hacker. Get you into trouble and make people blame you so you get kicked out of cyberspace, see? Or become too afraid to go online again."

Austin thought he understood.

"I did a pretty good job," said the clone, "don't you think?"

"Yeah, I guess you did." Austin still couldn't believe what he was hearing.

The clone held out his hand. "So. The transponder."

But Austin wasn't quite ready to give up his only trading piece. What would keep the clone from running off again, leaving him and Ash—

"Wait a minute. Where's my sister?"

"How would I know?" The clone looked around and shrugged again. "But you don't have to worry about her. She's probably here somewhere."

CHAPTER 22

Ashley's Plan

Oh, Ashley was there somewhere, all right. She tried not to breathe, afraid even the smallest noise would give her away. From her hiding place behind the stack of ruined virtual Van Gogh paintings, she listened quietly while Graffiti Guy played back a QuickTime video clip of Mr. Z telling him exactly what to do.

"I want you to tag as many murals or school projects or even Web sites as you can," the substitute teacher said. "Do everything you can to make it look like Austin Webster's doing. We want to get him off the Web and keep him off. Our work here is too important for him and his sister to interfere with."

Wow. Now she finally understood what was going on. And while Austin and…the other Austin argued about all the damage the digital clone had done, she thought through her plan.

Well, *plan* might have been too fancy a word for it. She

didn't have many options other than her brother's digital camera, snagged on her way into this mess of a site.

So what now? From what she'd gathered, Austin had accidentally sent his digital clone back into the Internet when he'd snapped his photo at the mural at school. Would it work in reverse? She looked down at the camera's silver control knob. Her heart pounded and her fingers shook a little. This *could* go wrong. She hoped she could hold the camera steady enough to take a decent picture.

But now was her chance, if she had a chance at all. So she took a deep breath and counted.

One: Hold camera overhead.

Two: Point and shoot at the two Austins.

Three: Download the shot. Quick!

Four: Pray!

Well, that should have done it. Maybe. She held the camera in her hand and listened to the whirring sound that told her something was happening. And when she realized she no longer heard the boys' voices, she peeked over the top of the paintings.

They were gone.

Whew. Ashley sighed. All that remained were the stolen bits of Web sites, with stuff like *Austin was here* spray-painted all over them. That and a floating QuickTime video screen replaying Mr. Z's confession over and over. *Shame no one can hear it back home. That would be helpful at the meeting with Mr. Hayward.* If Austin ever made it to that meeting, that is. Just because he and his clone had disappeared didn't mean they were home yet.

Ashley sure wasn't. Yes, she was glad they'd found the vandal, and she knew Austin could probably clean up most of the mess the guy had left online. But how would she get home? She couldn't just hold out the camera in front of her face, snap a photo, and send her *head* back to Normal. What about the rest of her?

"Too bad I can't find Mr. Z and ask him to take my picture." Of course she didn't mean a word of it. And now would be a very bad time for him to show up at his Web site of pirated stuff. She for sure couldn't leave the camera behind for him to find.

Ashley sneezed and buried her face in her hands. There had to be a way out of here. There just had to be. Her head throbbed.

"That horrible virus," she muttered.

A crash from behind a group of headless statues made her jump.

Yikes! Mr. Z?

Not quite.

"Did somebody say virus?" asked a familiar, high-pitched voice. "This is your virus protection program, Virus Patrol.

Give us ten minutes to sweep it all up, and we're out of here. Where is it?"

Ashley almost tried to hide behind the paintings again until it dawned on her what the guy had said. "Where do you take a virus," she asked, "once you sweep it up?"

"Back to Normal, obviously." The elflike character seemed to have no patience for questions as he and his buddies huffed around the site, looking for problems. "To Austin Webster's laptop, where the original host protocol is hyperlinked to a 23.7 gigahertz..."

Whatever it was sounded great, and Ashley smiled.

"Well, then, I'm your virus, fellas. Sweep *me* up."

As Austin's Virus Patrol got ready, she plugged her nose and took a final look around at the Pompeian statue, the wall mural, the paintings. And it occurred to her...

"Wait a minute." She glanced at the video of Mr. Z, replaying for the umpteenth time. "I wonder if we could bring a souvenir video home with us. Maybe I can use it for my project."

Or maybe for a private showing.

Ashley sneezed again, just for good measure.

The HyperLinkz Guide to Safe Surfing

Austin T. Webster here, and once again I had to rescue my sister after she got into trouble inside the Internet.

Ashley: Excuse me, but can you believe what he just said? My brother is never serious. I think everybody with two eyes can see who rescued whom this time.

Austin: Yeah, and they know where you were when I pulled you out—

Ashley: Okay, okay. Maybe we should call it even. But I'd like to explain a few things to people, if you don't mind.

Austin: Be my guest.

Ashley: Thank you. First, I want to remind everyone that most of the Web sites in the story are made up, though they're sometimes inspired by real ones. We'll let you know which ones you can visit in a minute.

Austin: Don't you feel like one of those voices at the end of a TV commercial when you say that? Void where prohibited. See participating dealer for details…

Ashley: I never thought about it that way.

Austin: Must be over eighteen. Not available in Alaska and Hawaii...

Ashley: You're funny. But let me go on. Remember how we visited a Web site about Pompeii, Italy? Pompeii was buried in AD 79 by a powerful eruption of Mount Vesuvius, just like in the story. The buried city site was rediscovered in 1748 and eventually dug up. Now it's like a time capsule of how people lived then. And, believe it or not, there was a lot of graffiti on the walls. Look it up in any encyclopedia *(try www.wikipedia.com)*, but please do be careful—graffiti can be rude.

Austin: Unlike me!

Ashley: Right... But actually, I'm not done talking about volcanoes. Because a horrendous eruption took place only a couple decades ago, in Washington State of all places. Mount St. Helens erupted on May 18, 1980, and you can learn more about it on dozens of Web sites—just type Mount St. Helens into your favorite search engine. Anyway, the blast covered many parts of the state—and beyond—with ash. It also completely choked Spirit Lake (where we were canoeing) with blown-down trees and worse. What a mess!

But the earth's volcanoes are nothing compared to those on Io, one of Jupiter's moons. In February 2000 the *Galileo* spacecraft made its closest flyby of that moon, taking lots of beautiful pictures. You can see some of them at *http://galileo .jpl.nasa.gov.* Of course, nobody ever spray-painted graffiti on the real probe!

And then there's the story of the mysterious handwriting on the wall (ever heard that saying?) at Belshazzar's palace. The weird handwriting told the king his time was up. His day was over, and big things were going to happen. Read more about this strange but true story in chapter 5 of the book of Daniel in the Bible.

Here's another example of handwriting on the wall, or on the door—the Wittenberg door, that is, where Martin Luther posted his ninety-five theses. No, he wasn't the only one who believed the Bible taught that people are saved through God's grace, not because of something we can do. But most people who look back at that date see October 31, 1517, as the day the church changed, and history with it.

August 28, 1963, was another history-changing day. That's when a man named after Martin Luther—Martin Luther King Jr.—delivered one of the most important speeches in U.S. history: "I Have a Dream." It was another kind of turning point, almost as explosive as a volcanic eruption. And looking back, we can see how Martin Luther King Jr.'s speech put words to the civil rights movement, the push to treat all people the same, no matter what the color of their skin. You can read his entire speech online at *www.usconstitution.net/dream.html.* Really, everybody needs to read this one. It's important stuff.

Bottom line? These two Martin Luthers stood up for what they believed in, no matter what the cost. And they both believed that when they followed God, truth would win.

Austin: Truth does win out, like it did when we showed Principal Hayward Mr. Z's video. Except Mr. Hayward never really got the part about how Mr. Z wanted to keep us "off" the Web, and he never told anybody Mr. Z was the one behind the vandalism. All he said was there had been a horrible mix-up and that I didn't do it. Brother!

Ashley: It doesn't matter, Austin. All that matters is Mr. Z's no longer subbing, we're repainting the mural, we're both back in school, and nobody blames you. Isn't it great to be out of trouble?

Austin: Out of trouble. Yeah. For now.

See ya,

Austin and Ashley

P.S. to parents: The Internet can be a lot of fun. But please make sure your child is surfing safely. That means being there for them. Know what they're accessing. And consider using a good filtering service or software since it can help you sidestep some nasty surprises. Though we can't tell you which filter is best for your family's needs, you might begin by checking out a great site called *www.filterreview.com*. It will give you many of the options so you can make a wise decision.

Please visit the author's Web site at *www.RobertElmerBooks.com* to learn more about other books he's written or to schedule him to speak to your school or home-school group.